Adam Mickiewicz

Master Thaddeus

The last foray in Lithuania - Vol. 2

Adam Mickiewicz

Master Thaddeus
The last foray in Lithuania - Vol. 2

ISBN/EAN: 9783337284879

Printed in Europe, USA, Canada, Australia, Japan

Cover: Foto ©Andreas Hilbeck / pixelio.de

More available books at **www.hansebooks.com**

MASTER THADDEUS.

MASTER THADDEUS;

OR,

THE LAST FORAY IN LITHUANIA.

BY

ADAM MICKIEWICZ.

An Historical Epic Poem in Twelve Books.

Translated from the Original

BY

MAUDE ASHURST BIGGS

(TRANSLATOR OF "KONRAD WALLENROD").

WITH A PREFACE BY W. R. MORFILL, M.A.

AND NOTES BY THE TRANSLATOR AND EDMOND S. NAGANOWSKI.

VOL. II.

LONDON:
TRÜBNER & CO., LUDGATE HILL.
1885.

𝔅𝔞𝔩𝔩𝔞𝔫𝔱𝔶𝔫𝔢 𝔓𝔯𝔢𝔰𝔰

BALLANTYNE, HANSON AND CO.

EDINBURGH AND LONDON

BOOK VII.

COUNCIL.

*The sound and salutary counsels of Bartek, called the Prussian
—The soldierly appeal of Matthew the Baptist—The politic
opinion of Buchman—Jankiel counsels a reconciliation, which
is severed by the Penknife—The speech of Gervasy, wherein
are exhibited the great effects of Diet eloquence—Protestation
of old Matthew—The sudden arrival of warlike rein-
forcements breaks off Council—"Down with Soplica!"*

In order due their Envoy Bartek now
Commenced his speech.   He, as he often went
On rafts unto the kingdom, had been named
The Prussian by his fellow-countrymen ;
In jest, for greatly did he hate the Prussians,
Although he loved to talk of them.   A man
Advanced in years, in his far journeys he
Had seen much of the world, a constant reader
Of the gazettes, well-versed in politics ;

In Matthew's absence he was usually
The president of council.

           " This is not—
Sir Matthias, my brother, and good father
Of all of us—this is no empty promise ;
I'd count upon the French in time of war
As on four aces.   'Tis a warlike people,
And since the days of Thaddeus Kosciuszko,
The world has ne'er seen such a martial genius
As the great emperor Bonaparte.   I well
Remember   when   the   Frenchmen   crossed   the
     Warta.
That time beyond the frontier I was staying,
During the year of eighteen hundred six.
I was with Dantzig trading, but I have
In Posen many relatives ; I went
To visit them ; and therefore with Pan Joseph
Grabowski, now commanding officer,
But who at that time in a village lived
Near Objezierz, I hunted some small game.
Peace then was in Great Poland, as is now
In Lithuania, but a sudden rumour
Spread all at once of a terrific battle.
An envoy sent by Todwen came to us.
Grabowski read the letter through, and cried

Out, 'Jena, Jena! The Prussians have been beaten
Upon the head, the neck! A victory!'
I, lighting from my horse, fell on my knees,
To thank the Lord. We rode into the town,
As though on business, as we knew of nought.
And there we saw the Landrath, Hofraths, all,
Commissioners, and all such sons of dogs.
They all bow low to us, each trembling, pale,
Like Prussian insects * deluged with hot water.
Rubbing our hands, and laughing, we entreat
Humbly for news; we ask, 'What news of
    Jena?'[1]
They marvelled that already we should know
Of their defeat; the Germans cry: '*Ach Gott!*
O weh!' They went back home, and from their
    houses
They ran as fast as feet could carry them.
Oh! what a scramble! all the roads were full
Of fugitives. The German folk like ants
Crawled fast away, the carriages ran on,
Which there the folk call *Wagen* and *Fornalken*,
Men, women, carrying pipes and coffee-pots,
And dragging pillows, feather beds; they hurried

---

* A name for black beetles, commonly called in Poland
" *szwaby* " or Swabians.

As best they might.   But we in silence went
To council; hey! on horseback, to confound
Retreating of the Germans ! Now to smite
The Landraths on the necks, and flog the Hofraths,
And catch the *Herren Offiziere* by
Their pigtails ! But our General Dombrowski
Did enter Posen, and he brought the Emperor's
Command to insurrection !   In one week
Our men so soundly had the Prussians thrashed,
And driven them away, thou couldst not get
A German, ev'n for medicine.   Suppose
We also should thus nimbly turn about,
And with such speed, and here in Litva make
Just such another bath for Muscovy.[2]
Ha! what dost thou think, Matthew? If the Russians
Contend with Bonaparte, it were no jest
To fight with him.   He is the greatest warrior
In all the world, and he has countless armies.
Ha ! what does Matthew think, our Father Rabbit?"

He ended.   All await old Matthew's sentence.
Matthew nor moved his head, nor raised his eye,
But only many times he struck his hand
Upon his side, as though he sought his sabre.
Though since the land's partition he had worn

No sabre, yet from ancient habit, when
He heard the mention of the Muscovites,
He moved his hand towards his left side aye,
As though to wield his Rod, and thence was he
Called Zabok.*   Now he lifted up his head,
They listen in deep silence.   But Matthias
Deceived the general expectation, for
A cloud hung o'er his brow, and once again
His head sank down upon his breast.   At length
He spoke, pronouncing slowly every word
With emphasis, and nodded to 't in time.

"Silence!" he said; "whence cometh all this news?
How far off are the French?   Who is their leader?
Have they begun already war with Russia?
Where, and for what?   And whence are they to
      march?
What is their strength?   What foot, and what of
      horse?
Who knoweth, let him speak!"

                              Then silent all
The assembly, gazing each on each.   "I gladly,"
The Prussian said, "would wait the Bernardine,

---

* *Za*, at or by, *bok*, side.

For the news comes from him.   Meantime we must
Send to the frontier trusty spies, and arm
The district all in secret ; and meanwhile
Conduct the whole thing prudently, so as
Not to betray our plans unto the Russians."

"Ha ! wait? and bark? put off?" a second
        Matthew
Broke in, the Baptist christened, from a great
Club, which he called the Sprinkler. 'Twas with him
To-day ; he on its body leaned both hands,
And on the handle did support his chin,
Exclaiming, "Wait ! delay ! hold *sejmiks* ! Hem !
Trem ! brem ! and then to fly !   I have not been
In Prussia ; kingdom reason's good for Prussia ;
But for me noble's reason.   This I know,
That whoso wants to fight, has but to grasp
A Sprinkler ; who will die, call in the priest,
And thus be quits !   I want to live, to be !
What is the Bernardine?   Are we then schoolboys?
What's Robak * unto me?   Let us be worms,
And on to gnaw at Muscovy !   Trem ! brem !
Spies, scouts !   Do you know, you there, what this
        means ?

---

* The worm.

It means you're old men, and incapable !
Brothers ! 'tis weasel's work to ferret out,
A Bernardine's to beg, but mine, to sprinkle !
To sprinkle, and be quits !"   And here he stroked
His club, and after him the crowd of nobles
Shouted full loudly, "Sprinkle, sprinkle, sprinkle !"

The Baptist's side supported was by Bartek,*¡
Surnamed the Razor, from his thin-edged sword,
Likewise by Matthew, who was named the Bucket,
From a great rifle which he bore, with throat
So wide that he from it, as from a pail,
Could pour a torrent of a dozen bullets.
Both shouted, "Long live Baptist with the
     Sprinkler !"
The Prussian tried to speak; his words were drowned
By tumult and by laughter; they exclaimed,
"Away ! thou Prussian ! coward ! he who is
A coward, let him hide himself beneath
A hood of Bernardine."
                    Old Matthew then
Slowly upraised his head, and then the noise
Began to cease a little.   "Mock not," said he ;

---

* Bartholomew.

" At Robak, 'tis a tough blade of a priest.
That tiny worm has gnawed a bigger nut
Than you.   I saw him only once, he scarce
Had cast a glance, I knew at once the game.
The priest did turn away his eyes, as fearing
That I should deign confess him.   But all that
Is no affair of mine ; there's much in this
To talk about.   He never will come here.
'Tis vain to call the Bernardine to us.
If all this news proceed from him, who knows
With what intent ?   A devil of a priest
It is !   If nought you know beside such news,
Why come you here, and what more do you wish ? "

" War ! " cried they.—" What war ? " asked he.
      They replied,
" War with the Muscovites ! To fight 'em ! Hey !
Down with the Muscovites ! " The Prussian shouted
Unceasingly, and ever raised his voice,
Until he gained a hearing, part by bowing,
And partly by his thin and noisy speech.

" I too desire to fight," he cried, and smote
With both hands on his breast ; " although I bear
No Sprinkler, with a barge-pole once I gave

Good christening to four Prussians at a time,
Who would have drowned me in the foamy Pregel."
" You're a bold fellow, Bartek ! " Baptist cried.
" Good !   Sprinkle,   sprinkle ! " — " But   then,
    sweetest Jesus !
We first must know with whom to fight, and why ;
Must tell it to the world," the Prussian cried.
" For who will follow us ? where shall they march ?
When, whither go, when we ourselves don't know ?
Brother nobility ! ye noble sirs !
Good gentlemen ! we must have judgment, we
Must order have and regularity !
Ye wish for war.   Let us confederate ; [3]
Let us consider how we shall unite,
And underneath whose staff.   So was it in
Great Poland ; we the Germans saw retreat.
What did we ?   We in secret did advise ;
We armed the nobles, and the peasant throng.
When ready, we did wait Dombrowski's orders ;
At last ! heyday ! to horse ! we rose at once."

" I beg a hearing," the Commissary *
From Klecko cried.   A young man, handsome,
    dressed

---

* German—*Commissarius*, a sort of agent.

In German fashion.   Buchman was he called.
But yet he was a Pole, in Poland born.
'Twas not for certain known if he descended
From nobles ; but none asked concerning that,
And all respected Buchman, as he served
A great lord, a good patriot was, and versed
In learning ; he from foreign books had learned
The art of husbandry, and with good order
Performed the administration of the lands.
From politics he sage conclusions drew,
By writings smooth and elegant could make
Himself renowned.   And therefore all were still
When he began to speak.   " I beg a hearing,"
Repeated he, and coughed three times ; he bowed,
And thus with sounding lips he clattered forth :

" The previous speakers, in their eloquent
Speeches, have touched on all the vital points,
And chiefest ; they have the discussion raised
Unto a higher standard.   Unto me
Remains alone to blow unto one fire,
These scattered thoughts and reasonings.   I have
        hopes
To reconcile all contrary opinions.
Two parts in the discussion have I marked,

Division is already made; I go
By this division. First of all, for what
Shall we make insurrection? in what spirit?
This is the first and foremost vital question
The second question doth concern itself,
With revolutionary government.
And this division is right excellent,
Only I fain would have it t'other way.
First to begin with government. As soon
As government I understand, therefrom
I may deduce its spirit and its aim.
So, as to government; as I glance o'er
The history of all humankind, what in it
Observe I? That the savage human race,
Scattered in forests, herd together, bind
Themselves together for their mutual
Defence; they this consider, and this is
The first of councils. Each one then lays down
A portion of his proper liberty
For general good; and this is the first statute,
From whence, as from a fount, all legislation
Doth flow. We therefore see that government
Is by agreement framed, proceeding not,
As some judge wrongly, from the will of God
But on a mutual contract government

The rather is supported, and division
Of powers is but a needful consequence."
" There you have contracts ! of Kiew or Minsk ! "
Old Matthew cried out ; " truly Babin rule !⁴
Pan Buchman, whether God sent us the Czar,
Or 'twere the devil, I'll not quarrel with you,
But only tell us how to oust the Czar."

"Ay ! that's the knotty point ! " the Baptist
        cried.
" If I might spring up to the throne, and with
My Sprinkler plash and wet the Czar, no more
By any contract would he aye return,
Of Kiew, of Minsk, or any Buchman treaty ;
Nor could his priests by power divine restore him,
Nor by the power of Belzebub.   I call
Him a bold fellow, who will sprinkle.   Buchman,
Your speech, good sir, was very eloquent,
But eloquence is froth and hum.   To sprinkle,
That's the chief thing."
                            " Just so, just so," hissed forth,
Rubbing both hands together, Bartek, named
Razor, from Matthew to the Baptist running,
Like shuttle thrown from one side of a loom
Across its length unto the further side.

" Only thou Matthew with the Rod, and thou
Matthew with club, agree ; by heaven ! we
Shall smash the Muscovites to bits ; the Awl
Will go beneath the orders of the Rod."

" Command is good," said Baptist ; " for parade,
One order in the Kowno brigade we
Had, short and pithy : ' Frighten, but yourselves
Be not afraid !   Fight, but surrender not.
March forward often, deal blows thickly round !
Whizz ! whizz !' "

               " Yes, those the orders are for me,"
Replied the Awl ; " why write an act ? waste ink ?
We must confederate ?   Why is all this coil?
Our Matthew be the Marshal, and the Rod
His staff."—" Long live," cried Baptist, " Weather-
    cock !"
The nobles answered, " Long the Sprinkler live !"

But in the corners rose a murmur, though
'Twas stifled in the midst ; 'twas seen the council
Was now divided in two parties.   Buchman
Said, " Never praise I unanimity ;
That is my system."   Some one else exclaimed,
" I lay my veto down !" [5] some from the corners

Re-echoed him.   At last a rough voice spoke :
The nobleman Skoluba late arrived.
"What's this here, you Dobrzynskis? what is doing?
And we, are we then outlaws?   When we were
Invited hither from our settlement,
And by the Klucznik Rembajlo Mopanku,
They told us that some great things should be
        done ;
Not only the Dobrzynski family,
But the whole district, whole nobility,
Therein should be concerned, and Robak talked
In a like manner, though he never finished,
And indistinctly spoke, and darkly he
Explained himself.   At last, the end of ends,
We rode here, and by couriers summoned all
Our neighbours.   And you are not here alone,
Masters Dobrzynski.   We are full two hundred
From various other farmsteads of us here.
So let us all take counsel.   If a Marshal
Be needed, let us all proclaim him, be
The ballot equal.   Live equality !"

Two Terajewicze then, four Stypulkowscy,
Three Mickiewicze cried aloud, " Long live
Equality !" Skoluba's side upholding ;

And Buchman meanwhile, " Unanimity
Were ruin !"—And the Baptist said, " We'll do
Without your help. Long live our Marshal,
    Matthew
Of Matthews! Hey! unto the staff!" Loud
    shouted
All the Dobrzynskis, " We entreat you !" but
The stranger nobles, " We permit it not !" *
So in two parties was the crowd divided,
Each nodding in defiance to the rest ;
One crying, " We permit it not !" the others,
" We do entreat you ! "
                But old Matthew still
Alone unmoving, in the centre sat,
And the sole head immovable was his.
There opposite to him the Baptist stood,
With both hands leaning on his club ; but round
His head he kept turning, leaning on its top,
Like to a gourd fixed on a lofty pole,
And forward now, now back, alternately
He nodded, and unceasing "Sprinkle, sprinkle !"
Exclaimed. Along the room unquiet Razor
Ran from the Baptist unto Matthew's bench.

---

* *Liberum Veto.*

The Bucket slowly passed across the room,
From the Dobrzynskis to the noblemen,
As though he would unite them.   One cried out
Unceasing, "Shave!" the other, "Deluge 'em."
Matthew was silent, but 'twas plainly seen
That he was angry.

             And this uproar raged
A quarter of an hour, when from amid
The heads of all the shouting crowd upsprang
A shining column high.   It was a rapier,
A fathom long, a whole span broad, and sharp
On either side; it was a Teuton sword,
Of steel of Nuremberg.   All silence kept,
Gazing upon the sword; who carried it
They knew not, but immediately they guessed.
"The Penknife!" they exclaimed; "long live the
      Penknife!
Hail to the Penknife! jewel of Rembajlo!
Hail to Rembajlo, Notchy-pate, Half-goat,
Mopanku!"

             Soon Gervasy (for 'twas he)
Pressed through the crowd into the chamber's midst,
And made the Penknife's blade to flash around;
Lowering the point in sign of a salute,
To Matthew said: "The Penknife bows unto

The Rod.   My brothers, nobles of Dobrzynski!
I come not here to counsel you in aught;
I'll only tell you why I brought you here,
And what to do, how do't, yourselves decide.
Ye know that long a rumour goeth round
The nobles' farmsteads, that great things shall be
Done in the world.   Friar Robak spoke of this.
Ye all know?"—"Ay! we know!"   they cried.
      "Good, good."
"'Unto the wise,'" pursued the orator,
With penetrating glance, "'two words suffice.'*
Is this not true?"—"Ay, true indeed," they said.
"When the French Emperor," the Klucznik spoke,
Shall march from there, the Russian Czar from
      there,
War follows 'twixt the Czar and Emperor.
Kings fall to loggerheads with kings, as is
The custom among monarchs.   And shall we
Sit still? When great folks other great men throttle,
Let us the lesser strangle, each his own,
From high to low, the great the great, the small
The small; as soon as we begin to strike

* "*Mondrej glowie dosc dwie slowie*," proverb: *Verbum sat. sap.*

Down falls the whole confederacy of knaves.
Thus flourish happiness and the Republic.
Is not this true?"—"'Tis true," they said, "as
     though
He read it from a book."—"True," did repeat
The Baptist; "sprinkle, sprinkle, and be quits!"
" I'm ready aye to shave," the Razor cried.
" Do but agree," the Bucket courteously
Entreated, "under whose command to go,
Baptist and Matthew!"   Buchman interrupted:
" Let fools agree.   Discussions never hurt
The public cause.   I beg you to be still.
Let's listen, for the cause hereby will gain.
The Klucznik from a new point will discuss it."
" Rather," the Klucznik said, " from my great age,
'Tis meet for me to think of weighty things.
To do that there's an emperor, there will be
A king, a senate, deputies.   Such things,
Mopanku, are in Krakow done, or Warsaw,
But not among us here in Dobrzyn.   Not
On chimneys with a piece of chalk are written
Confederation Acts, nor in a barge;
On parchment are they written.   Not for us
To write an act, for Poland has alike
Crown and Litvanian Writers ; our forefathers

Proceeded thus.   My business is to slay with
The Penknife."—" Mine to splash with Sprinkler,"
    said
The Baptist.—"And to pierce through with the Awl,"
Cried Bartek of the Awl, his slender sword
Producing.
          "All of us," the Klucznik said,
" I take as witnesses.   For did not Robak]
Say that before you in your house receive
Napoleon, you must sweep the dirt away?
Ye all heard that.   Do ye all understand?
Who traitorously slew the best of Poles?
Who robbed him, plundered, yet would wrest away
The remnant from the true inheritor?
Who is he?   Must I tell you ? "—" 'Tis Soplica.
The villain!" broke in Bucket.—"Fie! the tyrant!"
Hissed Razor forth.   " Then sprinkle him!" said
    Baptist.
" If he's a traitor," Buchman said, " then to
The gallows !"—" Down !" cried all, " down with
    Soplica !"

But here the Prussian dared to undertake
Defending of the Judge, and to the nobles
He cried, with lifted arms : " My brothers ! no !

Ah! no! by God's wounds! What is this new thing?
Sir Klucznik, are you mad? Were we then speaking
Of this? Because a man at one time had
A mad and outlaw brother, shall we then
Chastise him for his brother? That were Christian!
There is some plotting of the Count's in this.
To say the Judge was hard upon the nobles
Is falsehood! Heaven forbid that it were truth!
It is yourselves would summon him to law,
But he seeks concord with you. Freely he
Doth yield his own; he pays the mark beside.
He has a suit against the Count—what then?
They both are rich; let lord contend with lord.
What's that to us? The Judge a tyrant! He
Did first forbid the peasant to bow down
To earth before him, saying that was sin.
Not seldom at his house a company
Of peasants (I myself have seen) sit down ,
With him at table. For his peasantry
He pays the taxes, and it is not so
In Klecko, though you rule there, Master Buchman,
In German fashion. What! the Judge a traitor!
We have known each other from the lowest form.
Good was he as a child, and now the same.
He loveth Poland more than all things. He

Keeps Polish customs, and no entrance gives
To Russian fashions.   Oft as I return
From Prussia, wishing to wash off the German,
I go to Soplicowo, as the *centrum*
Of Polish manners ; there one may drink in
And breathe one's country.   Heaven forbid !
    Dobrzynskis !
I am your brother, but I will not let
The Judge be wronged, and this shall come to
    nought.
It was not, brothers, in Great Poland so.
What spirit and what concord ! dear to mem'ry !
None there with such a trifle dared to mar
Our council."

          "'Tis no trifle," said the Klucznik,
"To hang up rascals !"

            Louder grew the murmur.
Then Jankiel begged a hearing ; on a bench
He sprang, he stood, and raised above their
    heads
His beard like tavern-bush, that hung far down
Unto his girdle.   With his right hand he
Did slowly doff his cap of foxes'-skin,
And with his left composed again his gown
Disordered ; then his left hand he replaced

Upon his girdle, and thus made discourse,
With fox-skin *kolpak* bowing all round :

"Now, sirs Dobrzynski ! I'm a Jew myself.
The Judge to me is neither kith nor kin.
I honour the Soplicas as right good
Masters, and as my landlords ; I respect
All the Dobrzynskis likewise, all the Barteks,
And Matthews, all as neighbours very good,
And benefactors.   But I tell you this :
If you do any violence to the Judge,
'Tis very wrong.   Maybe you'll conquer, kill—
But the Assessors, and the Sprawnik ? *   Prison.
For in the Soplicowo village is
A band of soldiers, *Jägers* † all.   The Assessor
Is in the house, and if he only whistle,
They'll muster there, and come as though on
      purpose.
And what will be ?   If for the French you wait,
The French are still far off ; the way is long.
I am a Jew ; I nothing know of war ;
But I was in Bielica, where I saw
Jews from the very frontier ; and they say,

* See note 9 in Book III.
† German—Sharpshooters or Chasseurs.

The Frenchmen stand on the Lososna river,
And if there's war, 'twill not be till the spring.
Now, thus I say ; wait yet a little time.
The Soplicowo house is not a booth
That one can take down, put into a waggon,
And drive away ; the mansion as it stood
Will stand until the spring.   The Judge is not
A Jew upon a lease ; he will not fly ;
You'll find him there next spring.   And now, go
    home,
And do not talk aloud of what has been,
For talking is in vain.   And if it please
The noble gentlemen, I beg you come
With me.   My Sarah has a little Jankiel.
I will treat all to-day, and have great music.
I'll order bag-pipes, bass-viol, two fiddles—
And Master Matthew loves old July mead,
And a new mazurka ; I have new mazurkas,
And I have taught my boys to sing right well."

The generally belovèd Jankiel's speech
Went to their hearts ; a cry arose, a shout
Of joy, a murmur of consent went round
Behind the very house—when with the Penknife
Gervasy pointed unto Jankiel.

The Jew sprang down, he vanished in the crowd.
The Klucznik cried, " Away, Jew ! never thrust
Thy fingers between doors; this thee concerns not!
Because you trade, Sir Prussian, with a pair
Of miserable barges, that belong
Unto the Judge, you strain your throat for him.
Have you forgotten then, Mopanku, how
Your father floated down to Prussia twenty
Barges belonging to Horeszko, whereby
He did enrich himself and family ?
And even all of you, who are in Dobrzyn,
You old men may remember, you, young men,
Have heard, the Pantler was to all of you
A father and a benefactor.   Whom
Sent he commissioner to his Pinsk estates ?
'Twas a Dobrzynski.   Who were his accountants ?
Dobrzynskis.   And his stewardship, finances,
To none except Dobrzynskis did he trust.
Your interests he promoted in the courts ;
He got you bread of favour from the king ;
He sent your children, at his own expense,
To school to the Pijary fathers,[6] paid
Their board and clothing, and at his expense
Advanced them when grown-up.   Why did he this ?
Because he was your neighbour.   And to-day

Soplica's borders touch upon your frontier.
When did he ever aught of good to you ?"

"Nothing whatever," Bucket now broke in ;
"For from a petty noble he grew up,
And how he puffs himself with pride, faugh! faugh !
How lifts he up his nose !   Do you remember?
I asked him to my daughter's wedding.   I
Was drinking ; but he would not drink.   Says he,
' I cannot drink like all you noblemen ;
You nobles drink like fishes.'   There's a magnate !
A delicate dish of flour of Marymont ![7]
He drank not; down his throat we poured the wine.
He cried, 'You wrong me !'   Well then, wait a bit,
And from my Bucket I will deluge thee !"

"The wretch !" cried Baptist ; "oh! I'll sprinkle
    him !
My son, he was a prudent boy, but now
He is grown so stupid that they call him Bustard.*
The Judge is cause that he is such a fool.
I said, ' Why creepest thou to Soplicowo ?
If there I catch thee may the Lord defend thee !'

* *Sak* in the original.

Again he went to see Sophia, lying
In wait among the hemp.   I caught him, and
I laid about his ears at once ; he bleated
And whimpered, as he were a little boy.
' Father, although you kill me, I must go.'
And he kept whimpering.   ' What is the matter ? '
And then he told me that he loved Sophia,
He wished to look upon her.   I was sorry
For the poor fellow ; so unto the Judge
I said, ' Judge, give Sophia to the Bustard.'
He said, ' She's young as yet ; wait three years
        more.
See what she wish herself.'   The wretch ! he lied !
He's now betrothing her to somebody.
I've heard so.   I will creep in at the wedding,
And with my Sprinkler sanctify their couch."

" And shall such villain," said the Klucznik, " be
A ruler ? shall he ruin ancient lords,
His betters ? shall he make to perish both
Horeszko's name and race ?   Where in the world
Is gratitude ?   It is not here in Dobrzyn.
Brothers, you wish to fight the Russian Czar,
And fear to fight the house of Soplicowo.
You are afraid of prison.   Should I counsel

You unto murder ?   Heaven forbid it !   Nobles
And brothers, by the law I take my stand.
The Count in very truth has gained the suit,
Has gained already not a few decrees.
It but remains to put in execution !
So was it formerly.   The tribunal
Wrote a decree, the nobles would enforce it,
Most chiefly the Dobrzynskis ; and your glory
Thus grew in Litva.   You yourselves, Dobrzynskis,
In the Mysk foray fought against the Russians,
Led by Wojsilowicz, the Russian general,
And by a villain who was friend to him,
Wolk of Logomowicze.   You remember,
How we made Wolk our prisoner ; how we
     wished
To hang him on a beam, inside a barn,
Because he was a tyrant to the peasants,
As well as servant to the Muscovites.
But as those foolish peasants pitied him,
I had to spit him elsewhere on my Penknife.
I will not here recall you other raids,
Without a number, whence you always came
With booty and applause, as suiteth nobles.
Why speak of this ?   To-day the Count in vain,
Your neighbour, urges suit, procures decrees,

And none of you will the poor orphan help,
Heir of that Pantler, who so many fed.
No friend now has he ; only me, the Klucznik,
And this most faithful Penknife here of mine."
"The Sprinkler also," said the Baptist.   "Where
Thou art, Gervasy, there will I be too.
And while I have a hand, and it can plash,
Plash in my hand !   For two are two !   By heaven,
Gervasy mine, thou hast a sword, and I
My Sprinkler, and I'll sprinkle well, and thou
Shalt hew them down.   And so whizz ! whizz !
        plash ! plash !
And let them talk !"

                    "And here is Bartek too,"
The Razor said ; "my brothers won't reject me.
And when you lather, I will shave away."
" And I," the Bucket said, " will march with you.
And if we cannot make the rest agree
About the choice of Marshal, what are votes
And balls to me ?   Another sort of ball
For me."   Here from his pouch he drew a handful
Of bullets, and he clinked them in his hand.
" Here are the balls," he cried ; "into the Judge
With all the balls !"—" With you !" Skoluba cried ;
" We'll join with you ; wherever you are, we

Shall also be !   Long live the Horeszkos ! live
The Half-goats! Long the Klucznik live, Rembajlo !
Down with Soplica !"
                    Thus the eloquent
Gervasy drew all hearts along with him,
For each one had some grievance 'gainst the Judge,
As usual is with neighbours.   One complained
Of damage, one about a clearing, one
About infringement of a boundary ;
The rest were moved by envy of his wealth.
But hatred did unite them all ; they pressed
Around the Klucznik, lifting up on high
Their clubs and sabres.
                    Matthew, hitherto
Gloomy, immovable, now from the bench
Arose, and strode into the chamber's midst,
And planted firm his hands upon his sides,
And looking straight before him shook his head.
He raised his voice, and slowly every word
Pronounced, with   emphasis   and   weight: " Ye
        fools !
Ye fools !   And fools ye are !   Who cometh to
The mill may grind upon you !   So then, while
The council talked of Poland's resurrection,
The common weal, ye fools ! there were disputes

Among ye! Ye could not, ye fools! discourse
Together, nor in order, or appoint
A leader over you, ye fools! But let
One urge your private grievances, ye fools!
Then is there concord 'mid you! Get you gone!
For as I Matthew am, by many millions,
Hundred of many thousands, cartloads, tons,
Waggons, casks full of devils ! ! !—" 8

All were silent,
As struck by thunder, till a fearful cry
Arose behind the house, " Long live the Count!"
He entered, riding in the Matthews' farm,
Himself well armed; ten armèd jockeys followed.
The Count was mounted on a gallant steed,
Clad all in black; a wide cloak over all,
Nut-brown, of cut Italian, without sleeves,
Like a great veil, and fastened by a clasp
About the neck, did o'er his shoulders fall.
He wore a broad hat with a feather, and
He bore a sword. Round turning, with the sword
The assembly he saluted.

" Live the Count!"
They cried; " with him we'll live and die." The
    nobles
Peeped from the cottage windows, following

The Klucznik, pressing nearer to the door.
The Klucznik went out, and the crowd rushed forth
Behind him through the doors.   Matthias drove out
The others, closed the door, and drew the bolt ;
But looking from the window once again,
Said, " Fools ! "

        Meanwhile the nobles flocked around
The Count, and went into the tavern.   Now
Gervasy recollected former times.
Three girdles from their garments he commands
They bring him ; by them from the tavern vault
He dragged three casks ; the one containing mead,
The other *wódka*, and the third held beer.
He drew the bung out ; with a murmur spurted
Three streams forth ; one like silver white, the other
Red as a bloodstone, yellow was the third.
They in a threefold rainbow play on high,
And in a thousand barrels falling, hum
Within a hundred glasses.   Loudly shout
The noblemen ; some drink, some wish the Count
A hundred years ; all cry " Down with Soplica ! "

In silence Jankiel meanwhile had escaped
Upon a bare-backed steed.   The Prussian, likewise
Unheard, though still he eloquently spoke,

Tried to escape; the nobles him pursued,
Crying, he was a traitor.   Far apart
Mickiewicz stood, nor shouted, nor advised,
But from his mien that he some evil thing
Concocted, plain was seen.   So to their swords,
And hey!   He backward drew, and made a stand,
Leaning against the hedge, when to his aid
Sprang Zan and the three Czeczots.   After that
The nobles were dispersed; but in this stir
Two on the hand were wounded, one received
A cut upon the ear; the others mounted
On horseback.

          Then Gervasy and the Count
Arrange the ranks, distribute arms, commands.
At last all down the settlement's long street
Gallop, loud shouting, "Down, down with Soplica!"

NOTES TO BOOK VII.

1. *" We ask what news of Jena ?"*

The battle of Jena took place on the 14th October 1806, and on the 27th November Napoleon entered Posen.

2.   *" In Litva made*
Just such another bath for Muscovy."

To prepare a warm bath for any one is a proverbial expression, meaning to thrash him soundly. It is said to have originated in the rough and ready chastisement inflicted by Boleslaw Chrobry, the founder of Poland's historic greatness, upon certain of his recalcitrant subjects, whom the intercession of his queen Konilda had saved from death. But before granting their pardon the king, who at that time was in the bath, sent for the criminals, and gave them with his own hands a scourging so severe as to give rise to the above-quoted proverb.

3. *" Let's make confederacy."*

Poland is perhaps the only country that has enjoyed what may be called an organised right and constitution of revolt. A discontented minority would often unite under a marshal and other officers to form a confederacy, or organised association for resistance to the royal authority, or that of the Diet. The purpose of the confederacy was set forth by a written act, and the confederates appear to have been generally recognised as belligerents. A revolt organised by a confederacy was called a *rokosz*. In their deliberations all questions were settled by a plurality of votes, and not by unanimity, so that the veto, of sovereign importance in the Diet, was of no use here.

4. "*Rather Babin rule.*"

The Republic of Babin was a political satire devised in the reign of Sigismund I. (contemporary with Henry VIII.) In it all offices were purposely bestowed on those least qualified to fill them. The post of cellarer was given to a noted drunkard, that of chancellor to a man who could scarcely read or write. When the king inquired who possessed the royal authority, he was answered that during his lifetime the throne should be vacant!

The Contracts of Kiew and Minsk imply yearly meetings of landowners, farmers, or merchants, held in these principal cities for purposes of buying and selling. From the fact that many agreements are made at such meetings, the meetings themselves are termed *Contracts*. Those of Minsk are of little importance, but those of Kiew are still famous. They take place about the middle of February, and being the occasion of a great concourse of people, are in a measure equivalent to a season of business and gaiety combined. As these are the only contracts of which Matthias has heard, the word, as used by Buchman, naturally puzzles him.— E. S. N.

5. "*Veto.*"

"*Niepozwalam,*" the form in which the *liberum veto*, by which a single nobleman could annul the deliberations of a whole majority, was couched. It was not in use, until

first exercised by Sicinski of Upita, a nobleman of most
infamous character, in the reign of John Casimir (1648–68),
whence resulted a series of disasters, culminating in the
ruin of the country. The last exercise of the veto was by
Rejtan, as already noticed.

6. " *To school to the Pijary fathers.*"

The order of the Pijary monks (*Ordo Scholarum Piarum*)
attained, after the expulsion of the Jesuits in 1772, great
influence over the education of youth, and initiated, mainly
by the efforts of Konarski, an improved system of education.
While the Jesuits had laid the main stress upon Latin, the
Pijary substituted French as the groundwork of education.
This was an improvement upon the previous system, but it
had the effect of inducing an aping of French manners and
customs in literature and social life, till the reaction in favour
of Polish nationality.

7. " *A delicate dish of flour of Marymont.*"

The flour of Marymont, a small village near the gates of
Warsaw, is of a superior quality. The mill of Marymont is
celebrated as the place which served as a refuge to Stanislas
Augustus, after the attempt to seize him by the Confederates
of Bar, November 3, 1772.

8. "*By many millions,*" &c.

These three lines are not translated by me, but by Mr.
Naganowski.—M. A. B.

BOOK VIII.

———•———

THE FORAY.

The Wojski's astronomy—The Chamberlain's observations on comets—Mysterious scene in the Judge's apartment—Thaddeus, trying to extricate himself cleverly, gets into great trouble—The new Dido—The Foray—The last protestation by the Wozny—The Count captures Soplicowo—Storm, carnage—Gervasy as butler—The banquet of the foray.

BEFORE a storm a still and gloomy hour
Comes, while the cloud that soars o'er human heads
Stands still, and with a threatening countenance
Restrains the breath of winds; silent, it runs
Around the earth with eyes of lightning, marking
The spots whereon its thunders shall be cast
One after the other.   Now this hour of stillness
Came in the house of Soplicowo; well
One might suppose that some presentiment
Of strange events forthcoming, sealed all lips,
And raised all spirits to the land of dreams.

The supper o'er, the Judge and guests went forth
Into the court to enjoy the evening air;
They sit upon the banks all spread with turf.
The company, with still and gloomy cheer,
Looked up into the sky, which seemed to lower
Itself, and narrower grow, and evermore
To approach the earth; till both beneath the veil
Of darkness hidden, like a loving pair,
Began their secret converse, by their sighs
Suppressed their love confessing, by their whispers,
By murmurs, and by soft tones half aloud,
That formed a wondrous music of the evening.

The owl began it, from the gable-roof
Hooting; and with the rustling of their wings
The bats did whisper; near the house they flew
Where window-panes and human faces gleamed.
But nearer moths, the sisters of the bats,
Circled in swarms, lured by the garments white
Worn by the women; most they teased Sophia,
Striking against her face and her bright eyes,
Mistaking them for lights. And in the air
A mighty ring of insects gathered round,
Playing like spheres of an harmonica.
Sophia's ear distinguished, 'mid the thousand

Murmurs, the chord of humming of the flies,
And a false semitone the gnats created.

The evening's concert in the fields was scarce
Begun, for its musicians even now
Their instruments were tuning; now three times
The landrail screeched, the mead's first violin;
Now from afar the bittern's bass again
Re-echoed him from out the marsh; and now
The woodcocks, rising upwards, circled round,
And shrieked once, twice, as beating upon drums,
Finale to the murmurs of the flies,
And the birds' cries; a double chorus woke
Of two ponds, as among the Caucasus
Those lakes enchanted, silent in the day,
But musical at evening.   One pond, with
Bright water and a sandy shore, gave forth
A solemn low sigh from its azure breast.
The other pond, with muddy depths, and throat
More hoarse, replied with passionate grieving cry.
In both were singing countless hordes of frogs.
Both choirs were tuned unto two great accords;
One seemed *fortissimo*, the other soft
And *piano;* one appeared to cry aloud,
The other merely sighed; thus through the fields

Each pond held converse with the other pond,
Like two Æolian harps, that in their play
Answered each other.   Thicker grew the dusk,
And only in the grove, and round the osiers
Upon the brook, were gleaming wolfish eyes,
Like candles.   Far along the horizon's verge,
The fires of shepherds' camps gleamed here and
  there.
At last the moon uplit her silver torch,
She issued from the thicket, and illumed
Both sky and earth.   From twilight now unveiled,
They slept beside each other, like to happy
Consorts.   The heaven in its pure arms embraced
The bosom of the earth, by moonlight silvered.

Now opposite the moon one star, and then
Another, now a thousand gleamed, a million
Now twinkled; at the head of them shone bright
Castor, together with his brother Pollux,
Among the ancient Slavs called Lel and Polel,[1]
Now in the zodiac of the common folk
Re-christened; one named Litva, and the other
The Crown.*   The two Scales of the heavenly
  balance

---

* *i.e.*, Poland.

Shine further on ; the Lord, upon the day
Of the creation, as our old men tell,
Weighed all the planets and the earth in turn
Upon them, ere into the deeps of space
He launched their weights. The golden balance then
He hung in heaven ; therefrom men received
The model of their scales and balances.

Towards the north the starry circle shines
Of that famed Sieve,* through which the Lord, they
     say,
The rye-grains sifted, which from heaven he threw
To father Adam, banished from the garden
Of pleasure for his sin.
              A little higher
Stands David's chariot,† ready for career,
Its long beam pointing to the polar star.
The ancient Litvins of this chariot knew
That common people wrongly call it David's ;
It is an angel's car.   In it, ere time,
Rode Lucifer, when he defied the Lord,
And drove on headlong by the Milky Way
To heaven's threshold, until Michael hurled him
Down from his car, and cast it from the road.

---

* *Corona Borealis.*   † *Ursa Major.*

Now broken, doth it roll among the stars;
The Archangel Michael suffers not repair.
And this too know we from the old Litvini,
But they no doubt first learned it from the Rabbins,
That Dragon of the zodiac, long and great,[2]
Who winds his starry folds across the sky,
Whom sages wrongly have the Serpent called,
No snake is, but a fish, Leviathan.
Ere time he dwelt within the seas, but after
The deluge from the lack of water died.[1]
So angels hung him on the vault of heaven,
Partly for his strange figure, and in part
As a remembrance; they suspended there
His lifeless remnants, as the priest of Mir
Once hung up in his church the fossil ribs
And vertebræ of giants.[3]

            Such old stories
About the stars which he had learned from books,
Or from tradition knew, the Wojski told.
Although the ancient Wojski's sight was weak
At evening, and he could through spectacles
See nought in heaven, he knew by heart the names
And figures of each constellation there;
And so he pointed out their every place,
And orbit of their motion.

Few to-day

Listened to him, or heeded not at all
The Sieve, the Dragon, or the Scales.   To-day
A new guest, hitherto unseen in heaven,
Had drawn all eyes and thoughts unto itself.
This was a comet of first magnitude [4]
And power, that in the west appeared, and flew
Towards the north, and with a blood-red eye
Looked askance on the chariot, as it would
Assume the empty place of Lucifer.
It threw long tresses backward, and therein
Enwrapped the third part of the heavens, and
          gathered
As in a net a thousand stars,[5] and drew
Them after it, and measured ever higher
To northward with its head, and pointed straight
Up to the Polar star.

With unexpressed

Foreboding, the Litvanian folk each night
Gazed on this heavenly wonder, and therefrom
Deduced ill-omen, as from other signs.
For they too often heard the cries of birds
Ill-omened, who in flocks on desert plains
Gather, and whet their beaks, as they expect
Corpses.   Too often marked they how the dogs

Tore up the earth, and as though scenting death,
Howled fearfully, portending war or famine.
The guardians of the forest had beheld
The maiden of the pestilence pass through
The cemetery, she whose brow is high
Above the highest trees, and whose left hand
Waveth a bloodstained cloth.[6]

                Hence various
Conclusions drew, while standing by the hedge,
The barn-keeper, who came to give account
Of farm work, and the district writer, with
The bailiff whispering.

                But on the seats
Of turf before the house, the Chamberlain
Sat ; he broke in upon the guests' discourse.
It might be known he gathered voice to speak.
And his great snuff-box in the moonlight shone,
Entirely of pure gold, with brilliants set,
The portrait of King Stanislas in midst
Behind a glass.   He tapped thereon, took snuff,
And spoke thus : " Master Thaddeus, your talk
About the stars is but an echo of
The things you heard at school.   I much prefer
To talk of wonders with the ignorant.
I too attended lectures on the stars

Two years in Wilna, where the Puzynina,
A rich and learnèd lady, gave the rent
A hamlet of two hundred peasants yielded,
To purchase various telescopes and glasses.
Priest Poczobut,[7] a most illustrious man,
Was then observer, and of the Academy
At that time rector.   He, however, left
At last his chair and telescope, returning
Unto his convent, to his peaceful cell,
And there he made most exemplary end.
I likewise am acquainted with Sniadecki,[8]
Who is extremely learnèd, though a layman.
But your astronomers consider planets
Only as citizens may view a carriage ;
They know if to the capital it go
Before the king, or from the suburbs goes
Beyond the frontier ; but who rides therein ?
For what ? whereof he with the king discoursed ?
Or if the king has sent his envoy forth
With war, or as a messenger of peace ?
They know not.   In my time I recollect
How when Branicki * drove his chariot

---

* Xavier Branicki was the chief promoter of the Targowica and other conspiracies.

To jassow, and behind this wicked car
A train of Targowica traitors drew,
The train resembling of that comet there.
The simple people then, although they ne'er
In public councils mixed, at once could guess
That train the omen of some treason was.
'Twas said the people to this comet gave
The name of Broom, and said 'twould sweep away
A million."

        With a bow the Wojski answered,
"True, Most Illustrious, Powerful Chamberlain,
I recollect now what was told to me
Once as a little boy.   I recollect,
Though at that time I was not ten years old,
When in our house I saw the late Sapieha,[9]
Commander in the army, and who later
Became Court Marshal of the Crown, and died
At last Grand Chancellor of Litva, aged
A hundred and ten years.   He, in the time
Of John the Third, was at Vienna under
The standard of the Hetman Jablonowski.
Well then, the Chancellor related how
When John the Third on horseback mounted, when
The Papal legate blessed him on the way,
And when the Austrian ambassador

Did kiss his feet, and held the stirrup ready—
Count Wilczek the ambassador was named—
The king exclaimed, " See what is doing in
    heaven ! '
They looked : behold, a comet sailed o'erhead,
By that same way whereby Mahomet's armies
Marched on, from east to west.   And later on
Priest Bartochowski wrote a panegyric
Upon the triumph of Krakow, by the title
Of *Orientis Fulmen*, saying much
About this comet.   I have likewise read
About it in the work *Janina* titled,
Where is related the whole enterprise
Of the late King John, and where there is engraved
The standard of Mahomet, and besides
That comet, as we see this one to-day."

" Amen," the Judge said, " I accept your omen ;
May John the Third be with the star revealed !
Now in the west there is a mighty warrior ;
May be the comet brings him here to us,
Which Heaven grant !"
               Thereto the Wojski said,
Bending his head down sadly, " Comets sometimes
Mean war, and sometimes quarrels.   'Tis not good,

It shows itself right over Soplicowo ;
May be it threatens us some home misfortune.
We yesterday had strife and jar sufficient ;
The Regent had a quarrel with the Assessor
That morning, in the evening Master Thaddeus
Called out the Count.   This quarrel also came
About the bear's hide ; if the good Judge had not
Prevented me, I had made both disputants
Agree at table.   For I wished to tell
A singular adventure, very like
The events of yesterday's excursion ; it
Chanced to the foremost hunters of my time,
The envoy Rejtan and to Prince Denassau.
The accident was this :

                 " The General
Of the Podolian lands went from Volhynia,
To his estates in Poland, or indeed,
If rightly I remember, to the Diet
In Warsaw ; on his way he visited
The nobles, partly for amusement, partly
For popularity, and so he came
To Thaddeus Rejtan, now of holy memory,
Who later was our Nowogrodek envoy,
And in whose house I grew up from a child.
Now Rejtan, on the General's arrival,

Invited guests.   There gathered many nobles.
There was a theatre, for the Prince loved theatres
Kaszyc, who dwelt in Jatrze, fireworks gave ;
Pan Tyzenhaus sent dancers, and musicians
Oginski and Pan Soltan, who then lived
In Zdzienciele.   In a word, they gave
An entertainment in the house past wonder,
And in the forest was a grand hunt made.
'Tis known to you that nearly all, so far
As I remember, of the Czartoryskis,
Although proceeding from Jagellon blood,
Are little apt at hunting, not indeed
From idleness, but from their foreign tastes.
And the Prince-General more often looked
On books than on the kennel, and more often
On ladies' balconies than on the woods.

" But in the Prince's suite there came the German
Prince Denassau, of whom 'twas said that when
He sojourned in the Libyan land, he went
A-hunting, and he there a tiger * slew
With spear in single combat, and of this
A mighty boasting Prince Denassau made.

----

* A *tiger* in *Africa !!!*

We hunted at this season the wild boar.
Rejtan a monstrous sow killed with a rifle,
At great risk, since he fired from very near.
Each of us marvelled at the shot, and praised.
The German Denassau alone did hear
These praises with indifference, and muttered,
'A clever shot needs only a bold eye,
But steel a bold hand,' and began to brag
At length about his Libya and his spear,
About his negro kings, and of his tiger.
And Rejtan took this very ill; he was
A man of temper quick; he struck his sabre,
And said, 'Sir Prince! whoever looketh bold,
Should boldly fight; a wild boar's worth a tiger,
A sabre worth a spear;' and they began
A conversation over-warm.   But then
The General happily broke in on them,
And, speaking French, he made them to agree.
What there he said I know not, but it was
Only as ashes laid upon hot coals,
For Rejtan took this much to heart; he waited
Only an opportunity, and promised
To make the German pay for this.   Well-nigh
He paid with his own life for this offence,
And did it on the morrow, as I'll tell."

Here ceased the Wojski, and his right hand
    raised,
And for his snuff-box asked the Chamberlain.
He long time used it, and deigned not to end
His story, as he thought thereby to sharpen
The listeners' curiosity.   At last
This curious story he resumed ; they listened
With fixed attention ; but again the tale
Was broken off.   For some one to the Judge
Had sent a messenger, to say that he
Was waiting with some business very urgent,
Which might not be deferred.   Good-night then
    giving
To all the assembly, took the Judge his leave.
They parted and went divers ; some to sleep
Inside the house ; the others in the barn
Among the hay.   Then went the Judge to give
An audience to the traveller.

                The rest
Already slept.   But Thaddeus crept along
The passages, and like a sentry paced
All up and down before his uncle's door,
For he in weighty matters must request
His counsel ere he sleep.   He dared not knock ;
The Judge had locked the door, and secretly

Conversed with some one.   Thaddeus waited till
The end should come, and listened at the door.

He heard within a sobbing.   Stirring not
The latch, he gazed, with careful heeding, through
The keyhole.   There he saw a wondrous thing,
The Judge and Robak kneeling on the ground,
Embracing, while they wept with bitter tears.
Robak the hands was kissing of the Judge,
The Judge embraced the priest upon the neck,
And wept.   At last, a quarter of an hour
Being past while they kept silence, Robak spoke
These words in a low voice :
                              " The Lord knows, brother,
I hitherto have kept those secret vows,
Which I in sorrow made, beneath the seal
Of absolution ; that all consecrate
To God and to my country, serving not
Pride, neither seeking earthly glory, I
Have lived till now, and I have willed to die
A Bernardine, discovering not my name ;
Not hiding from the vulgar only, but
From thee and mine own son.   Yet from the
    Father
Provincial I had leave, in case of death,

To make full revelation of my name.
Who knows if I return alive ?   Who knows
What may occur ?   In Dobrzyn, brother, is
Great, great confusion.   Still the French are far ;
The winter must pass by ; we still must wait,
But nothing can withhold the nobles.   I
Perhaps was far too busy with this rising ;
Perhaps they understood me ill.   The Klucznik
Has spoilt it all.   That madman Count, I hear,
Hastened to Dobrzyn.   I could not forestall
        him,
There is a weighty reason why I could not,
For old Matthias has recognised me ; if
He lets the secret out, I then must give
My neck unto the Penknife.   Nothing will
Restrain the Klucznik.   'Tis but a small matter
About my head, but such discovery
Would break the whole web of conspiracy.
But yet I must be there to-day, to see
What they are doing, even though I die.
Without me all the nobles will go mad.
Farewell to thee, farewell, my dearest brother !
I must make haste.   If I should perish, thou
Alone must breathe a sigh forth for my soul
In case of war, the secret unto thee

Is known,—do thou complete what I began.
Remember ever, thou art a Soplica!"

The priest here dried his eyes, composed his frock,
Drew down his cowl, in silence opened wide
The window at the back, and from the window
He sprang into the garden; left alone,
The Judge sat in an arm-chair, and he wept.

A moment waited Thaddeus, ere he stirred
The latch; the door was opened, and he entered
In silence, and low bending, said, " Good uncle,
A few days scarcely have I tarried here.
These days passed like a minute. I have not
Had time sufficient to enjoy thy house
And presence; yet I now must ride away,
And hasten, even to-day, my uncle, and
Be far away to-morrow. You indeed
Remember we the Count have challenged. 'Tis
My business to fight with him; I have sent
The challenge. Duelling in Litva is
Forbidden; I will go unto the frontier
Of Warsaw's Duchy. Though the Count indeed
A coxcomb is, he has no lack of courage,
He'll surely come unto the place assigned.

We will arrange our meeting, and as fitting
I'll punish him, if Heaven prosper me.
Then from the shores of the Lososna I
Will swim the stream, upon whose farther shore
Our brothers' ranks await me.   I have heard
My father's testament commanded me
To serve in the army, and I know not who
This testament has cancelled."

                                  Said the uncle :
" My Thaddeus, are you in boiling water,
That thus you twist round like a hunted fox,
Who wags his tail one way, but runs another ?
We sent a challenge truly, and 'tis fitting
To fight ; but why such haste ? why go to-day ?
The usual custom is, before a duel,
To send a friend, and make conditions.   Then
The Count may beg our pardon, deprecate.
You wait a little ; there is time enough,
Unless some other demon drives you hence.
Tell me sincerely, why so roundabout ?
I am your uncle, and though old, I know
What young hearts are ; I have been to thee a
        father "—
This saying, he stroked him underneath the chin—
" My little finger has already whispered

Something of this to me, that you have some
Affairs among the ladies—hang it ! now
Young men take quickly to the ladies !   Well,
Thaddeus, confess it all to me, and truly."

"True," stammered Thaddeus ; "true ; some
     other reasons
There are, dear uncle ; 'tis my fault perhaps.
An error ! a misfortune ! hard to mend.
Dear uncle, no, I dare no longer stay.
A fault of youth ! My uncle, ask no more !
I must from Soplicowo part in haste."

" Ho !" said the uncle, "love disputes no doubt !
I marked how yesterday you bit your lips,
While looking on a certain little girl
Askance.   She also had, as I perceived,
A little pouting mien.   I know these fooleries !
How when a pair of children are in love,
'Tis sorrow measureless ; they now rejoice,
Now are cross and sad.   Heaven knoweth why,
     they quarrel
Both tooth and nail ; now, sulking in their corners,
They will not speak to one another, even
Sometimes they run away into the fields.

If this has chanced to you, I'll take on me
To reconcile you soon.   I know these fooleries;
I once was young.   So tell me all, and I
May also in my turn discover something.
We both will make confession."

                              " Uncle," then
Said Thaddeus, as he kissed his hand, and blushed,
" I'll tell the truth entirely.   This young lady,
Your ward, Sophia, pleased me very much,
Although I have but seen her twice.   They say
You mean the daughter of the Chamberlain
To be my wife; she is beautiful, and is
The daughter of a rich man, but I cannot
Marry Miss Rosa when I love Sophia.
It's hard to change one's heart, nor would it be
An honourable act, to marry one
And love another.   Time may be will cure me,
I'll ride away from here for a long time."

" Thaddeus," broke in the uncle, " this to me
Seems a strange way of loving, from the loved
To fly.   'Tis well for thee thou art sincere;
Thou seest thou wouldst have done a foolish thing
If thou hadst ridden off.   What shouldst thou
    say

If I myself betrothed Sophia to thee?
What! dost not jump for joy?"
Said Thaddeus,
After a while had passed: "Your goodness, sir,
Astonishes me. But how can it be?
Your favour is of no avail to me,
For all my hopes, alas! are but in vain,
For Madam Telimena will not give
Sophia to me."
"We will entreat her," said
The Judge.
"No, no one can prevail with her,"
Did Thaddeus answer; "no, I may not tarry.
Dear uncle, I must quickly ride away,
To-morrow, uncle; give me but thy blessing.
I have prepared all things; I'll ride at once
Unto the Duchy."
Twirling his moustache,
The Judge with anger looked upon the boy.
"So this is thy sincerity? 'tis thus
Thou openest thy heart to me? At first
This duel, then 'tis love, and this departure!
Fie on it! In this is some complication.
They have talked to me, and I have tracked your
    steps.

You are a libertine and a deceiver !
You have told me lies ! Where went you yesterday ?
Why like a weasel crept you near the house ?
O Thaddeus, if you could deceive Sophia,
And now will fly, young man, you shan't succeed.
Love or not love, I tell in truth to you,
That you shall wed Sophia, and to-morrow
You stand upon the carpet.*   And if not,
Stripes ! Talk to me of feelings, changeless heart !
Thou art a liar ! I will find out all
About you, Master Thaddeus ; fie upon you !
I'll give you a good scolding even yet.
I have had enough of trouble in the day,
Until my head does ache ; and still this fellow
Will not allow me yet to go to sleep.
Go you to bed ! " This saying, he opened wide
The door, and called the Wozny to undress him.

In silence Thaddeus went, with drooping head,
This painful conversation with his uncle
In thought discussing. 'Twas the first time he
Had been so harshly chidden ; yet he felt
The justice of this sharp reproach. He blushed

* *Stanąc na kobiercu,* an idiomatic expression for the
ceremony of marriage.

Before his very self.   What should he do?
What if Sophia should hear of this?   Entreat
Her hand?   And what would Telimena say?
No, he must stay no more in Soplicowo.

Thus deep in thought he scarce had gone two steps,
When something crossed his path; he stopped, he
    saw
A phantom all in white, long, slender, thin.
She glided towards him with her outstretched hand,
From whence the trembling moonlight back was
    thrown,
And coming near, low sighed she, "Thankless man!
Once thou didst seek my glance, thou shun'st it
    now.
Thou didst my conversation seek, but now
Dost close thine ears, as though within my words,
And in my looks, a deadly poison lurked.
'Tis well, I know thee what thou art—a man!
Unknowing coquetry, I had no wish
To torture thee.   I made thee happy; thus
Wouldst thou repay me?   O'er a heart too soft
This victory has made thy heart too hard.
Because thou hast too easy conquest made,
Thou dost despise my heart too soon!   'Tis well!

But, taught by such experience, credit me,
Far more than thou canst do, I scorn myself."

Said Thaddeus, " Telimena, Heaven forbid
My heart were hard, or that I should avoid thee
From scorn ; but thou thyself consider this,
They spy upon us, track our steps.   Can we
Thus openly ?—What will be said ?   It were
Unsuitable.   By Heaven, it were a sin."
" A sin ? " she answered, with a bitter smile.
" Thou innocent ! thou lamb ! I, though a woman,
Care not about a love-affair, although
I were discovered, though I were dishonoured.
And thou, thou art a man !   What injury
To one of you, although he should confess
To having with ten women all at once
Love passages?   Speak thou the truth, dost thou
Wish to abandon me ? "   She burst out weeping.
" But, Telimena, what would the world say,"
Spoke Thaddeus, " of the man, who at my age,
In these days, being sound, in the country lived
And loved, when now so many youths, so many
Ev'n married men from wives and children part,
To go beyond the frontier, and to gather
Beneath the nation's standard ?   Though I should

Desire to stay, does that depend on me?
My father in his testament ordained
That I should in the Polish army serve,
And now my uncle this command repeats.
I go to-morrow, my resolve is fixed,
And Heaven forbid that I should change it now."
" I," Telimena said, "would not obstruct
Thy path to glory, nor thy fortunes mar.
Thou art a man, thou'lt find a love more worthy
Thy heart; one richer, fairer, thou wilt find.
But let me only for my comfort know,
Before our parting, that thine inclination
Towards me was true love.   That 'twas not only
A jest, no vain debauch, but love indeed.
Let me but know my Thaddeus loves me still!
Let me the words, 'I love,' hear from thy lips,
Let me engrave them on my heart, and write them
Within my thought.   More easily will I
Forgive thee, even if thou cease to love,
Remembering how thou once didst bear me love."
Here she began to sob.
                              Thaddeus was moved
To pity, seeing how she wept, and prayed
So tenderly, and asked so small a thing.
The purest grief and pity him possessed;

And had he searched his spirit's inmost depths,
He had not known for certain, if or no
He loved her.   So he spoke with earnestness.
"May I be struck by lightning, Telimena,
If 'tis not true I liked thee very much,
Or loved, by Heaven !   Short the moments were
That we together spent, but they for me
So sweetly passed, so dear they are, that long
They will be ever present to my thought,
And Heaven forbid that I forget thee aye."

Then Telimena sprang upon his neck.
" I hoped for this," she said ; "thou lovest me,
Therefore I live.   For I to-day did purpose
To end my life with mine own hand.   If thou,
My dear one, lov'st me, canst thou cast me off ?
I have given my heart to thee ; my property
I'll also give thee ; I will follow thee
To every place ; each corner of the earth
Were sweet to me with thee ; the wildest desert,
Believe me, love will change into a garden
Of pleasures."
                    Thaddeus released himself
By force from her embrace.   "What !" answered he,
" Art thou in thy right mind ? where ? and for what ?

To follow me? I, but a private soldier,
To take thee with me, as a *cantinière?*"
" We will be married," answered Telimena.
" No, never ! never !" answered Thaddeus.
" I have no intent at all to marry now,
Or love. That was but nonsense, let it be.
I pray thee, love, consider, be at peace !
I am grateful to thee, but I cannot wed thee.
Let us each other love,—but thus,—apart.
I may no longer tarry ; no, no, I
Must go. Farewell now, Telimena mine,
To-morrow I shall go."

                      He spoke, and pressed
The hat upon his brows, and turned aside,
Wishing to go, but Telimena stayed him
With glance and visage of Medusa. He
Must tarry 'spite himself, and looked in fear
Upon her form ; she stood, unbreathing, still,
And lifeless, till she stretched her hand forth like
A sword for piercing, with the finger aimed
Straight at the eyes of Thaddeus. " I desired
This man !" she cried ; "ha ! tongue of dragon !
    ha !
Thou heart of lizard ! Was it nothing, then,
That I, infatuate with thee, have scorned

The Assessor and the Regent, and the Count?
Thou didst deceive me, and now leav'st forlorn!
That's nothing, for thou art a man! I know
Your wickedness! I knew that, like the rest,
Thou couldst break plighted faith; I did not know
Thou couldst so basely lie!   I listened at
Thine uncle's door.   And so this child, Sophia,
Has pleased thine eyes, and treacherously thou
Pursuest her?   Thou scarcely hast deceived
One hapless woman, 'neath her very eyes,
Thou seekest a new victim!   Fly, but yet
My curse shall overtake thee; or remain!
Thy wickedness I'll publish to the world!
Thine arts no others shall deceive, as they
Did me deceive!   Away! I scorn thee, thou
A liar art, a vile man!"

                        At this outrage,
Deadly to noble's ears, which no Soplica
Had ever heard with patience, Thaddeus shook;
Pale as a corpse his visage, on the ground
Stamping, and pressing close his lips, he said,
"Thou foolish woman!"

                        He departed; still
This term of "vile" re-echoed in his heart,
And the youth shuddered; well he felt that he

Deserved it, felt that he had done great wrong
To Telimena, that she had with justice
Chastised him.   Thus to him his conscience spake,
Yet more he loathed her for these accusations.
And oh, Sophia ! he dared not think of her,
It caused him shame !   Yet this Sophia, so fair,
So sweet, his uncle had to him betrothed her ;
She should have been his wife, if Satan still,
Entangling him from sin in fresher sin,
In falsehood after falsehood, had at last
Left him with laughter, chidden, scorned by all.
He had wasted all his future in two days !
Alas ! this was the just reward of crime !

In this wild storm of feelings, suddenly
That duel gleamed before him like an anchor
Of rest.   " I'll slay that villain Count ! " he cried
In anger ; " I will have revenge or die ! "
But wherefore slay ?   Himself he could not tell ;
This rage exceeding, as it had possessed him,
So in a twinkling did it blow away.
Again deep grief possessed him, and he thought,
" If true be my surmises that the Count
May have some understanding with Sophia—
What then ? Perhaps the Count loves Sophy truly.

May be she loves him, will for husband choose him.
What right have I to break such marriage off,
Myself unhappy, others' bliss destroy?"

He fell into despair, and saw no help
But rapid flight, and where? but to the grave.

So pressing hard his fist upon his brow,
He rushed into the meadows where the ponds
Gleamed far below, and o'er the muddy pool
He stood.   He plunged his greedy glance into
The green gulf, and inhaled its muddy odour
With pleasure, and he opened wide his lips
Towards the pond.   For suicide is aye
In choice as delicate as all debauch;
And he in the mad whirling of his brain,
Felt unexpressed attraction to the mud,
To drown himself therein.
                                    But Telimena,
Who from the youth's wild looks had guessed the
        depth
Of his despair, beholding him thus rush
Towards the ponds, though she with anger glowed
Against him, and this justly, she was frightened
For him, she was in truth kind-hearted.   Though

She deeply grieved that Thaddeus should dare
To love another, she would punish him,
But not destroy.   So rushed she after him,
Exclaiming, "Stay! most foolish! Love or not!
Marry, or ride away; but only stop!"
But he in rapid flight outran her far,
And stood now on the border of the pond.

By strange decree of fate, on this same shore
The Count now rode, with all his jockey troop,
And by the beauty of so fair a night,
And by the wondrous harmony of that
Sub-aqueous orchestra, charmed; those choirs
That sounded like Eolian harps—no frogs
Can make such music as the Polish frogs—
He stayed his horse, and his emprize forgot.
Turned to the pond, he listened curiously.
His eyes roved o'er the fields, and heaven's wide
        plain,
In thought composing landscapes of the night.
The neighbourhood indeed was picturesque,
The two ponds with their visage near approached,
Like two fond lovers; waters smooth and clear
The right-hand pond presents, like maiden's cheeks.
The left-hand pond seemed something darker, like

The swarthy visage of a youth, bedecked
Already with the down of manhood.   One
Glittered with golden sand, like shining locks ;
The forehead of the second pond with osiers
Seemed bristling, and a tuft of willows bore.
Both ponds were garmented in robes of green.

From them two streams, like hands together clasped,
Gushed forth.   The stream of these united fell
Down to the vale ; it fell, but was not lost,
For in the darkness of the trench it bore
Upon its waves the gilding of the moon.
The water fell by stages, and on each
Shone handfuls of the moonlight.   In the trench
The light was shivered into tiny fragments ;
The fleeting current caught them, and them bore
Away into the depths, and from above
Again the moonlight still in handfuls fell.
Thou wouldst have said a Switezianka [10] sat
Beside the pond, and with one hand did pour
The water from a vessel bottomless,
While with her other hand she flung, in sport,
Handfuls of gold enchanted, from her lap
Into the water.   .
           Further, from the trench

The stream escaped meandered o'er the plain,
Silent, but one might see its current flow ;
For on its moving, trembling surface, bright
The shimmering moonlight sparkled all its length,
Like the fair Samogitian serpent, called
Givoitos ;[11] which, although it seems to sleep,
Lying among the heather, crawleth on,
As it by turns with gold and silver gleams,
Till sudden from the eye it vanishes,
In moss and fern.   The stream, meandering thus,
Lay hid among the alders, shadowy black
Upon the horizon's verge, their forms upraising
Light, scarcely to the eye expressed, like spirits
Half on the earth, half in the clouds beheld.

Between the two ponds sat within the trench
A mill half-hidden, like an ancient guardian
Spying upon the lovers, listening
Their conversation ; seized with anger, he
Spreads wide his arms, and shaking head and hands,
Doth stammer threats.   Thus suddenly the mill
Now shook his moss-grown brow, and whirled
    around
His many-fingered fist, loud-clattering,
And stirred his toothèd wheels; thereby he drowned

The loving conversation of the ponds,
And roused the Count from out his reverie.

The Count, perceiving Thaddeus had approached
So near his warlike station, cried, " To arms !
Seize him ! "   At once the jockeys sprang to earth.
Ere Thaddeus might be well aware what chanced,
They captured him.   Towards the house they rush,
They entered in the courtyard, woke the household ;
Loud barked the dogs, and sentries shouted loud.
The Judge half-dressed came forth ; he saw a crowd
Of men well armed, and thought them robbers, till
He recognised the Count.   " What means all this ? "
He asked.   The Count his sabre brandished o'er
        him,
But seeing him disarmed his rage grew cool.
" Soplica," said he, " thou eternal foe
Unto my family, I will chastise thee
To-day for recent and for ancient crimes.
So do me justice for my fortune's plunder,
Ere I revenge me for my honour's wrong."

But making sign of cross, the Judge replied,
" In the name of Father and the Son ! Sir Count,
Fie, fie ! are you a robber ?   Heaven forbid !

Is this becoming to your noble birth
And breeding, and your high rank in the world?
I will not let myself be wronged!"   Just then
Up rushed the servants of the Judge, some armed
With sticks, with rifles others.   Standing far
The Wojski gazed with curiosity
In the Count's eyes, but in his sleeve concealed
A knife.   Now had begun a fight; the Judge
Prevented this, however.   'Twere in vain
To make defence; for newer enemies
Arrived upon the scene; among the alders
They saw a gleam, the light of rifle shots.
The bridge across the stream resounded loud
With horses' hoofs, and "Hey! upon Soplica!"
A thousand voices cried.   The Judge did shudder:
He knew Gervasy's signal.   "This is nothing,"
The Count said; "more of us will soon be here!
Surrender, Judge, for these are my allies."

Then rushed the Assessor, crying, "I arrest you
In name of his Imperial Majesty.
Yield up your sword, Sir Count, or I will call
For military help; and know you, sir,
That whoso ventures an assault by night,
By the twelfth hundred ukase is apprised,

That like an evil "—— Here, upon his face
The Count with sword-flat struck him, and the
    Assessor
Fell stupefied, and in the nettles lay.
All thought he had been wounded, or were dead.

" I see," the Judge said, " your intent is murder."
All cried aloud.   Sophia's shrieks o'erpowered
The others ; clasping close the Judge, she screamed,
Like child transfixed with needles by the Jews.*

Meanwhile, among the horses Telimena
Proceeded, and towards the Count outstretched
Her claspèd hands.   " Upon thine honour," cried
    she
With piercing voice, with head thrown back, with
    hair
Streaming, " By all things holy, we implore thee
Upon our knees !   Count, darest thou refuse ?
The ladies pray thee !   Cruel one, thou first
Must murder us ! "   She fell down in a swoon.
The Count sprang forth to help her, much
    surprised,

---

* The mediæval fable and excuse for persecution.

And somewhat troubled by this scene. "Miss
    Sophy,"
He said, "and Madam Telimena, ne'er
This sword shall be defiled by guiltless blood.
Soplicas! ye are all my prisoners! Thus
Did I in Italy, when underneath
That rock the Sicils call Birbante-Rocca,
I captured the intrenchments of the robbers;
Those armed I slew, commanded to be bound
The unarmed; they behind our horses went,
And decked my glorious triumph; after that
We hanged them at the base of Etna's mount."

This was a happy chance for the Soplicas,
The Count, possessing better horses than
Those of the noblemen, and wishing first
To engage the enemy, had left them far
Behind, and by a mile * at least outran
Their cavalry, and with his jockey train,
Obedient and used to discipline,
He had some sort of army regular,
While all those nobles, as insurgents wont,
Were stormy, and most prompt to hang their foes.

---

* The Polish mile is equivalent to between two and
three of English.

The Count had time to cool from his first rage,
And thought how fitliest he might end the war
Without the need of shedding blood.   So then
He gave commandment to imprison all
The household of Soplica in their house,
As prisoners of war, and at their doors
He posted sentries.

      Then "Down with Soplica!"
Arose.   The nobles in tumultuous crowd
Rushed in; besieged the mansion, and by storm
Took it; the easier because the leader
Was captive, and the garrison dispersed.
But yet the victors longed to fight; they sought
For foes, and not admitted to the house,
They ran to the farm buildings, to the kitchen.
When they the kitchen entered, there the sight
Of pots, the fire extinguished scarce, the fresh
Odour of food, the crunching of the dogs
Gnawing the remnants of the supper, took
All hearts, and quickly changed the thoughts of all;
It cooled their rage, and kindled need of food.
Tired by their march and council all day long,
Three times they cried in concert, "Eat, eat, eat!"
"Drink! drink!" arose the answer. Thus there were
Two choruses, some calling out for food,

For drink the others.   Loud the uproar still
Re-echoed ; where it only reached it caused
All mouths to water, and with hunger moved
Each one ; at signal given from the kitchen,
The army all dispersed for foraging.

Gervasy, from the Judge's rooms repulsed,
Respecting the Count's sentinels, must yield
Perforce.   So as he might not there take vengeance
Upon his enemy, he thought upon
The expedition's second great intent.
Like an experienced man and versed in law,
He would install the Count all legally
In his new heritage, and formally.
The Wozny he pursued, and after long
Searching, he spied him hid behind the oven.
He collared him, and to the courtyard dragged
And to his breast the Penknife holding, said :
" The Count, Sir Wozny, ventures to entreat
That you will deign proclaim forthwith, before
The brother nobles, this his intromission
Upon the castle, and Soplica's mansion,
The village, seedlands, fallows ; in a word,
Cum grovis, woodis, et boundariebus,[12]
Peasantis, atque rebus omnibus,

Et quibusdam aliis.   As thou
Knowest, so bark thou, leave thou nothing out."

" Sir Klucznik, wait awhile," Protasy said
Boldly, his hands upon his girdle laid ;
" I am ready from all parties to fulfil
Commands, but I must warn you that such act,
By violence extorted, will possess
No force in law, proclaimed too in the night."
" What violence is there ? " said the Klucznik ;
        " here
Is no assault.   I rather courteously
Entreat you.   If it seems unto you dark,
I with my Penknife will a fire upraise,
That speedily shall glimmer in your eyes,
As though in seven churches."—" Old Gervasy,"
The Wozny said, " why makest thou such haste ?
I am a Wozny ; it is not my business
To sift the action.   It is known to you,
A party will bespeak a Wozny, and
Dictate to him the thing they will, and he
Proclaims it.   He is herald of the law,
And none may chastise heralds.   Therefore I
Know not why thus you hold me under guard.
I presently will write an act ; let some one

Bring me a lantern here.   But I meanwhile
Proclaim: Be silent, brothers!"
                                        And to speak
With greater clearness, mounted he upon
A mighty pile of beams, that underneath
The orchard hedge were heaped to dry.   He climbed
Upon the pile, and all at once, as though
The wind had blown him off, he from their eyes
Had vanished.   'Mid the cabbages they heard him;
They saw among the dark hemp his white cap
Flit like a pigeon by.   The Bucket fired
Thereat, but missed his aim.   The hop-poles now
Began to crackle ; now Protasy walked
Among the hops.   "I do protest," he cried,
Certain of his escape, for him behind
The bed and marshes of the streamlet lay.

After this protestation, which had sounded
As the last cannon shot o'er conquered ramparts,
Ceased all resistance in Soplica's house.
The hungry nobles plundering went around,
And gathered what they might.   The Baptist made
His quarters in the cattle-shed, and sprinkled
One ox and two calves on the head.   And Razor
Had in their throats his sabre buried deep.

The Awl had used with equal diligence
His little sword, and pierced some sucking pigs
Beneath the shoulder-blades.   Now carnage threat-
    ened
The birds.   The watchful geese, who one time saved
Rome from the treachery of Gauls, now cackled
In vain for help.   Instead of Manlius,
The Bucket enters in their roost, he strangles
Some of the birds, and to his girdle binds
The others living; vainly, with hoarse throats,
The geese cry out; in vain the hissing ganders
Nip the invader with their beaks; he forth
Rushes, with down all covered, that in flakes
Falls, thick as sparks.   By motion of their wings
Borne   on,   as   though   by   wheels,   he   seemeth
    Chochlik,
The wingèd evil sprite.

                          But fiercer carnage,
Although less noisy, 'mid the poultry raged.
Young Bustard entered in the hen-house; there,
Mounting by ladders, caught with ropes, and drew
Down from above the cockerels, crested hens,
And tufted; strangled each one after each,
And threw them in a heap. Most lovely birds,
Nourished on pearly groats !   O heedless Bustard !

What impulse thus did urge thee ?   Nevermore
Will prayers of thine appease Sophia's wrath.

Gervasy now remembered former times.
He ordered *kontusz* girdles to be brought,
And thereby from Soplica's cellar drew
Casks of old spirits, liquors, and of beer.
He drew the bungs from some, the others seize
The noblemen ; with ready will, as thick
As ants, they roll them to the castle ; there
The whole crowd gather for the night ; the Count
Has there made his headquarters.

       They now lay
A hundred fires, they boil, they roast, they fry;
The tables bend beneath the load of meat,
Drink flows in rivers.   All the noblemen
Would eat, and drink, and sing this whole night
  through ;
But gradually they began to sleep,
And yawn ; eye is extinguished after eye,
And all the assembly nods ; each where he sat
Falls down ; the one falls with a dish, the other
Over a kettle, one by a beef quarter.
Thus sleep, death's brother, has the victors
  vanquished.

NOTES TO BOOK VIII.

1. "*Lel and Polel.*"

Two legendary twin princes, whose story forms part of the powerful, though fantastical drama of "Lilla Weneda," by Julius Slowacki.

2. "*That Dragon of the zodiac, long and great.*"

I should not like to say positively, but I am *almost* certain that the appellation *Smok* does not exist even in Polish manuals of astronomy. It may be, however, that such is the name in Lithuania for scorpion, or that the poet, not being able to introduce the idea of a scorpion, used dragon. None of the twelve zodiacal signs seem to answer the description, except *Scorpio*. It may be *Serpens* in Ophiuchus.—E. S. N.

3. "*Once hung up in his church the fossil ribs
   And vertebræ of giants.*"

* It was customary to hang up in churches fragments of fossil bones, which the people supposed to be those of giants.

4. *" This was a comet of first magnitude."*

The famous comet of 1811, which, having been scarcely visible during April and May, reappeared with great splendour, after passing its perihelion, in August, the date of this story, and remained visible all the autumn. The tail on October 14 was estimated at 100,000,000 miles long, and 15,000,000 broad ; the head measuring 1,270,000 millions of miles. Its period is supposed to be 3000 years.

5. *" And gathered*
As in a net a thousand stars," &c.

The comet of 1811 is described as having its tail divided into two streams, parting from the head, and again united into a curve at their base ; so the image used is both characteristic and descriptive.

6. *" Whose left hand*
Waveth a bloodstained cloth."

The common people of Lithuania figure the Pestilence under the form of a maiden of gigantic stature, and waving in her hand a bloodstained cloth, from which she scatters the pestilence. The appearance of this spectre is commonly supposed to precede the ravages of the plague, or other epidemic. (See notes to " Konrad Wallenrod.")

The comet of 1811, besides being regarded as an evil omen in Poland and Russia, received in Spain the name of " El Cometa de Hambre," as preceding a great famine, that immediately followed on the Peninsular war.

7. *" Priest Poczobut,"* &c.

* The priest Poczobut, an ex-Jesuit, published a work on the Zodiac of Dendera, and by his observations assisted Lalande in calculating lunar motions.

8. "*I likewise am acquainted with Sniadecki.*"

John Sniadecki (1756–1830), a famous astronomer, and writer on scientific subjects. From 1807 to 1825 he was professor of astronomy and rector of the University of Wilna. Among other places he studied some time at Oxford.

9. "*The late Sapieha.*"

The family of Sapieha furnished several distinguished men during the seventeenth century, and especially during the reign of John Sobieski.

10. "*A Switezianka.*"

The Wilias, Switeziankas, Rusalkas, are the water-maidens of popular Lithuanian legend.

11. "*Like the fair Samogitian serpent called Givoitos.*"

These snakes were formerly objects of worship, in the old paganism of the country.

12. "*Cum grovis,*" &c.

The original is a species of legal macaronic Latin; an imitation of the same effect has been attempted by means of English words, similarly Latinised.

BOOK IX.

———

THE BATTLE.

Of the danger resulting from disorderly camping out—Unex-
pected succour—Sad situation of the nobles—A begging
friar's rounds are an omen of rescue—Major Plut by exces-
sive gallantry draws a storm on himself—A shot from a
pocket-pistol the signal of war—Deeds of the Baptist, deeds
and danger of Matthew—The Bucket saves Soplicowo by an
ambush—Cavalry auxiliaries, attack on infantry—The
deeds of Thaddeus—Duel of the leaders, interrupted by
treachery—The Wojski by a decisive manœuvre turns the
scale of war—The bloody deeds of Gervasy—The Chamber-
lain a magnanimous victor.

AND in such sound sleep lay they that they woke not
At shine of lanterns, nor the entering
Of several men, who fell upon the nobles
As those wall-spiders named scythe-spiders pounce
On flies half-sleeping. Scarcely one may buzz,
With lengthy legs its cruel conqueror
Embraces it around, and strangles it.
But sounder than the sleep of flies, the sleep

Was of the nobles ; not one buzzed ; they all
Lay there as lifeless, though by powerful arms
Seized, and rolled over like to packs of straw.

Alone the Bucket, who no equal owned
In all the district for his strength of head
At banquets, could two firkins drink of mead
Ere his tongue tripped him, or his legs him failed,
Though he had feasted long, and deeply slept,
Gave yet some sign of life.   He oped one eye,
And saw—true nightmares.   Two most dreadful
     faces
Right o'er him ! each a pair of whiskers bore.
He felt their breath, their whiskers touch his lips,
They move their fourfold hands like wings around.
Afraid, he tried to sign the cross ; in vain
Would raise his hand, the right hand pinioned
     seemed ;
He moved the left ; he felt, alas ! the spirits
Had bound him like an infant swathed in bands.
He feared things yet more dreadful, oped his eyes,
And lay unbreathing, stiff, and all but dead.

But yet the Baptist strove to save himself.
It was too late ! already he was fastened

In his own girdle; yet he writhed about,
And made such powerful springs, he fell upon
The sleepers' chests, among their heads he rolled,
And like a pike-fish flung himself about,
Who throws him on the sand, and like a bear
He roared aloud, for he had powerful lungs.
He roared out "Treachery!" The whole assembly
Waked up, and all in chorus answered, "Treachery!
Violence! and treachery!"

                    To the mirrored hall
The echoes of that shout arrived, where slept
The Count, Gervasy, and the jockeys.   Then
Gervasy woke, in vain he strove to rise,
To his own rapier bound in stick-like form.
He looked, and through the window armèd men
Perceived, in low black hats, green uniforms.
Of these one, girded with a scarf, upheld
A sword, and with its point his company
Of soldiers ordered, whispering the while,
"Bind! bind!" Around like sheep the jockeys
      lie
In bonds; the Count sits unbound, but disarmed;
Beside him stand, with naked bayonets,
Two soldiers. These Gervasy recognised.
Alas! they are Muscovites!!

　　　　　　　　　　　Not seldom had
The Klucznik been in such a plight before.
Not seldom ropes were on his feet and hands,
Yet could he free himself; he knew the way
To break asunder bonds; great strength had he,
Trust in himself; in silence he considered
How best release himself.　He closed his eyes,
As though he slept; he slowly lengthened out
Both feet and hands, drew in his breath, compressed
His chest unto the narrowest, until
At once contracting, swelling, rolling up,
As when a serpent hides both head and tail
Among his folds, Gervasy thus from long
Grew short and thick; the ropes expanded, they
Did even creak, but still they did not burst.
The Klucznik turned him round in shame and rage,
And on the ground his angry visage hid;
Eyes closed, he lay insensible as wood.

Then woke the drums: at first full low, and then
With ever greater and with louder rattle.
At this *appel* the Russian officer
Ordered the Count and jockeys to be locked
Within the hall, and under guard, to lead
The nobles to the mansion, where there stood

The second band.   In vain the Baptist strove,
And flung himself about.

                The staff was placed
Within the mansion, and with it were many
Well-armed nobility, Podhajscy,
And Birbaszowie, Hreczechy, Biergele,
Relations all, or friends unto the Judge,
Who hastened to his succour when they heard
About the attack, the more because they long
Had been at feud with the Dobrzynskis.

                        Who
The Muscovite battalion from the hamlets
Had brought ?   Who from the nobles' farmsteads
    round
So fast had summoned all the neighbourhood.
The Assessor was it ? or else Jankiel ?
Of this were differing tales, but no one knew
For certain, either then, or later on.
Now had the sun arisen, all bloody red,
Stripped of his beams, half seen, and half in clouds
Concealed, like horse-shoe in a smithy's coals
Enkindled.   Now the wind increased, and blew
Clouds from the eastward quarter, thick and ragged
Like ice-floes ; every cloud cold drizzly rain
In flying scattered ; after it the wind

Flew swift, and dried the rain up; and again
A damp cloud following the wind rushed on.
And thus the day by turns was chill and rainy.

Meanwhile the Major ordered to be brought
Some beams that near the house were laid to dry,
And in each beam with hatchet to be cut
A half-round opening, and in these holes
To insert the prisoners' legs, and close them round
With other beams.　Both logs of wood, with nails
Secured upon the corners, tightly pressed
Like canine jaws upon their legs; their hands
Were tighter yet secured behind their backs.
The Major, to increase their torment, ordered
Their caps to be first stripped from off their heads,
Their cloaks from off their shoulders, their *kontusze*,
Ev'n *taratatki*, even their *zupany*.
And thus the nobles, fettered in the stocks,
Sat in a row, their teeth all chattering,
In cold and rain, for still the wet increased.
In vain the Baptist strove, and flung about.

In vain the Judge made intercession for
The noblemen, and Telimena joined
Entreaties to Sophia's tears, to use

Towards the prisoners greater gentleness.
The officer, indeed, who led the band,
Nikita Rykow, though a Muscovite,
A good man,[1] let himself be pacified.
But what of that when he must Major Plut
Himself obey ?
        This Major was by race
A Pole from Dzierowicz, and named, 'twas said,
In Polish Plutowicz ; but he had taken
Another name ; a rascal great was he,
As usual with a Pole who makes himself
A Muscovite in service of the Czar.
Plut with his pipe stood there before the front,
With hands upon his side ; and when folks bowed
To him, he lifted up his nose in air,
And for all answering he blew as sign
Of angry humour from his mouth a cloud
Of smoke, and went away into the house.

But meantime had the Judge made Rykow mild,
And led the Assessor likewise on one side,
Consulting how to finish this affair
Without a trial, and, yet more important,
Without entanglement with government.
So Captain Rykow said to Major Plut,

"Sir Major, what to us are all these prisoners?
Must we deliver them unto the law?
'Twill be a great misfortune to the nobles,
And none will give you, Major, aught for this.
Major, do you know how we'll best compose
This business?   Let the Judge reward your pains.
We'll say that we came here a-visiting,
Thus will the goats be whole, the wolf be fed.
It is a Russian proverb, 'All things can
Be done, if but with prudence.'   And a proverb
Is this, 'Roast on the Czar's spit for yourself.'
And this too is a proverb, 'Better is
Agreeing than disagreement,' 'Weave thou well
The knot, and put the end in water.'   We
Need give in no report, so none need know.
For 'God gave hands to take'—a Russian proverb."

This hearing, up the Major starts and snorts
With anger: "Rykow, are you mad?   This is
The imperial service, service is not friendship.
Stupid old Rykow!   Are you mad?   Shall I
Let mutineers loose, in these warlike times?
Ha! ha! you Poles! I'll teach you mutiny!
You miserable nobles! you Dobrzynskis!
Eh! I'll soon teach you!   Let the wretches soak!"

He roared with laughter, from the window looking.
"Why, there's that same Dobrzynski in a surtout!
Hey! strip him of his surtout! last year he
Began at a redoubt this quarrel with me.
And who began it? He it was, not I.
He, when I danced, exclaimed, ' Put out that thief!'
For I was then accused of pilfering
The regimental chest, and undergoing
Examination, and in mighty trouble.
But what was that to him? As I was dancing,
He cried behind me ' Thief!' the noblemen,
' Hurrah!' They wronged me; what then? In
      my claws
This wretched nobleman has fall'n. I said,
' Eh! what! Dobrzynski, eh! " The goat has come
Unto the waggon." ' What, Dobrzynski, now?
Thou seest it may come unto a flogging!"

Then to the Judge he whispered in his ear,
"Judge, if you wish the affair to pass off well,
For every head pay down a thousand roubles *
In ready cash; a thousand roubles, Judge.
That's the last word."

* About £166.

The Judge to bargain tried;
The Major would not hear; about the room
He walked, and belched thick smoke, as does a
    squib
Or rocket; while the women followed him,
Weeping and praying.   "Major," said the Judge,
"What will you gain, if you do summon us?
There here has been no bloody fight, there were
None wounded; as they ate the hens and geese,
According to the statute, they must pay
Full compensation.   I'll bring no complaint
Against the Count; that only was a common
Quarrel of neighbours."

                    "Judge," the Major said,
" Have you yet read the Yellow Book?"—"What is
The Yellow Book?"[2] the Judge inquired.—"A
    book,"
The Major answered, " better than your statutes;
For every other word therein is, 'ropes,
Siberia, knout!' the book of martial law,
Proclaimed now through all Litva; your tribunals
Are now beneath the table.*   For a trick
Like this, according to our martial law,

---

* Equivalent to "at a discount."

You'll get hard labour in Siberia
At least."—" I will appeal," the Judge replied,
" Unto the governor."—" Appeal," said Plut,
" Even to the Emperor.   You know that when
The Emperor confirms a ukase, often
He through his clemency the penalty
Increases twofold.   You appeal ; perhaps
I'll find out in necessity, Sir Judge,
A good hook ev'n for you ! For that spy, Jankiel,
Whom long the government has watched, he is
Your servant, dwelling in your tavern.   Now
I can arrest you all together."—" Me ! "
The Judge exclaimed ; " arrest me ! How will you
Dare without orders ? "   And the quarrel grew
Ever more violent, when at once arrived
A new guest in the courtyard.
                              A tumultuous
Arrival 'twas.   First as some wondrous courier,
A monstrous black ram entered ; with four horns
His head was bristling, whereof two like arches
Were twisted round his ears, and decked with bells,
And two, whose ends protruded from his brows,
Shook balls, round, brazen, clattering.   After him
Came oxen, and a flock of sheep and goats ;
Behind the beasts four heavy laden wains.

All guessed it was the entrance of the friar.
The Judge, who knew the duties of a host,
Stood on the threshold to salute his guest.
The priest upon the foremost carriage rode ;
The hood half hid his visage, but they quickly
Did know him, for as he the prisoners passed,
He turned his face to them, and beckoning made.
The driver of the second car likewise
They knew ; old Matthew 'twas, the Rod, disguised
In peasant garments ; soon as he appeared
The nobles raised a shout.   He said, " Ye fools ! "
And with his hand commanded them be still.
The third the Prussian bore in ragged coat,
And Zan and Mickiewicz were in the fourth.
Meanwhile Podhajscy and Isajewicze,
Birbasze, Wilbikowie, Biergicle,
Kotwicze, seeing the Dobrzynski nobles
In this harsh slavery, began to cool
Down from their former anger by degrees ;
For Poland's nobles, though most quarrelsome,
And very quick to fight, are not vindictive.
So they for counsel to old Matthew haste.
He stations the assembly round the cars,
And orders them to wait.

      The Bernardine

Then entered in the room ; they hardly knew him,
Although not changed in dress, for he had taken
Upon him such a different mood.   By custom
Gloomy and thoughtful, now he raised his head,
And with a cheerful mien, like jovial friar,
Ere he began to speak, laughed loud and long.

" Ha ! ha ! ha! I salute you, ha ! ha ! ha !
Most excellent ! first-rate !   Sir officers,
Whoever hunts by day, you hunt by night.
Good hunting ! I have seen the game.   Ay, ay !
Pluck, pluck the nobles, strip 'em of their husks !
Ay, put a bit on 'em, for they are skittish !
I must congratulate you, Major, on
Catching the little Count.   'Tis a fat morsel,
Rich, and a young lord from his ancestors.
Don't let him from the cage, without you get
Three hundred ducats, and when you have got it,
Give some three farthings to the convent, and
To me, for I'll pray always for your soul ;
As I'm a Bernardine, I often think
About your soul.   Death seizes by the ears
Even staff-officers.   Well Baka wrote,[3]
' Death lurks behind the executioner
In scarlet, and not seldom soundly knocks

Upon the coat, and smites on linen as
Upon a hood, on frizzled locks as on
The uniform.'   Says Baka : ' Mother Death
Is like an onion, since she forces tears
Where'er she presses ; but unto her breast
She folds alike the child that will be lulled,
And the roaring bully.'   Ah ! ah ! Major, we
Do live to-day, to-morrow die.   That only
Is ours that we to-day may eat and drink.
Sir Judge, perhaps it's time for breakfast now ?
I'll sit at table, and beg all to sit
With me.   Some *zrazy*,* Major ?   Sir lieutenant,
What think you ?   If we had a bowl of punch ? "

" True, father," both the officers replied,
" 'Tis time to eat, and drink the Judge's health.'

The household wondered, as they gazed on Robak,
Whence he derived such mien, and merriment.
The Judge then gave these orders to the cook :
Bowl, sugar, bottle, *zrazy*.   All were brought.
Rykow and Plut did labour with such will,
Devoured so eagerly, and drank so deep,

* See note 19 to Book II.

In half-an-hour of *zrazy* twenty-three
They ate, and emptied half a mighty punch-bowl.

The Major, satiate and merry, hurled
Himself into an arm-chair, drew his pipe out,
And lit it with a bank-note; with a napkin
He wiped his breakfast from his lips, and turned
A laughing look upon the women, saying,
" I like you, pretty ladies, as dessert ;
And, by my epaulettes of Major, when
A man has eaten breakfast, after meat
The nicest relish is a talk with ladies,
Pretty as you, fair ladies !   I know what.
Let's play at cards, at *welba-cwelba*,[4] whist,
Or—a mazurka ! ha ! three hundred devils !
Am I not best mazurist in the first
Regiment of *Jägers*."   Therefore to the ladies
He bent half double, and by turns blew out]
Tobacco-smoke and compliments.]

        " A dance ! "
Cried Robak; "as I empty out a bottle,
I, though a priest, at times tuck up my gown,
And dance mazurkas !   But you know this,
  Major,
We here are drinking, but the *Jägers* freezing

Behind the house. Drinking is drinking. Judge,
Give 'em a whisky cask. The Major will
Allow this; let the valiant *Jägers* drink."
" I'd ask it," said the Major, " but herein
Is no compulsion." — " Give 'em, Judge," did
  whisper
Robak, " a cask of spirits." And thus, while
The merry staff were swilling in the house,
Behind it, drinking in the ranks began.

In silence Captain Rykow drained his cup.
But at the same time as he drank, the Major
Made to the ladies compliments; and ever
The zeal for dancing greater in him grew.
He threw away his pipe, and seized the hand
Of Telimena; he would dance, she fled.
So went he to Sophia, and bending double,
Invited her to a mazurka. " Here,
You Rykow, leave off puffing at your pipe ;
Put down that pipe, for you can play the lute.
Don't you see that guitar ? come, take it up.
Play a mazurka. I, the Major, will
Make one in the first couple." So the Captain
Took the guitar, began to screw the strings.
But once more Telimena asked to dance.

" Upon a Major's word, Miss, I'm no Russian.
I'll be a dog's son, if I'm telling lies.
If I tell lies—inquire ; the officers
Will witness all, and all the army says it,
That in this second army, the ninth corps,
The second foot division, fifteenth regiment
Of *Jägers*, Major Plut's the best mazurist.
So come along, Miss, don't be obstinate,
Or like an officer I'll punish you."

This saying, he sprang, seized Telimena's hand,
And on her pale arm gave a smacking kiss ;
When Thaddeus, springing from one side, bestowed
A blow upon his face.   The kiss and blow
Together sounded, one behind the other,
As word may follow after word.

                        The Major
Was all confounded, rubbed his eyes, and pale
With anger, cried, " Rebellion ! mutineer !"
And drawing his sword, made haste to pierce his
    foe.
Then from his sleeve the priest a pistol drew ;
" Fire, Thaddeus," he cried, " as at a candle."
Quick Thaddeus seized it, measured aim, and
    fired.

He missed, but stupefied and singed the Major.
Up started Rykow with his instrument.
"Rebellion !" cried he, and on Thaddeus rushed.
The Wojski brandished from behind the table
A knife held backwards.   Through the air it hissed
Between the heads, and sooner struck than gleamed,
It struck the depth of the guitar, the inside
To outside turning.   Rykow bent aside,
And thus avoided death, though much frightened.
Exclaiming, "*Jägers*, mutiny, by heaven !"
He drew his sword, and making good defence,
Drew near the threshold.

                    Presently there entered
From the other side the room, and through the
    window,
A many nobles, armed with rapiers, led
On by the Rod.   Plut reached the hall, and
    Rykow
Behind him ; they the soldiers call; already
Three nearest to the house as succour haste.
Now through the doors three gleaming bayonets
Creep in, and after them three low black hats.
With Rod uplifted Matthew in the doorway
Stood, leaning 'gainst the wall; he lay in wait
Like cat that watches mice, till fierce he smote,

And may be the three heads had rolled on earth;
But either the old man's sight served him ill,
Or over-great his ardour; ere they gave
Their necks to him, he smote upon their hats;
He tore them, but the Rod, down falling, clashed
On bayonets; the Muscovites drew back,
And Matthew drove them out into the court.

There the confusion was still greater. There
Soplica's partisans with emulation
Worked at unfettering the Dobrzynskis, tore
The stocks asunder. Seeing this the *Jägers*
Rush to their swords, and hasten to the place.
A sergeant with a bayonet pierced Podhajski,
Wounded two other noblemen, a third
He shot at, and they fled. The Baptist still
Was in the stocks; with hands already free,
Ready for combat he arose, upraised
His hand, and doubled up his lengthy fingers,
And from above upon a Russian's back
So fierce he smote, he brow and visage beat
Into the carbine's lock. The lock was stirred,
But drenched in blood the powder kindled not.
The sergeant rolled o'er at the Baptist's feet
Upon his weapon. Baptist bent him down,

And seized his rifle by its barrel.   Whirling
The rifle like his Sprinkler round, high raised,
Round turning like a windmill's sails, at once
He on the shoulders smote two rank and file,
And knocked a corporal upon the head.
The rest in terror drew back from the stocks.
Thus Baptist with a moving roof protected
The nobles.

   After breaking of the stocks,
And cutting ropes, the nobles being free,
Now fell upon the waggons of the friar,
And from them drew forth rapiers, sabres, swords,
Firearms, and scythes. The Bucket found two guns
There, with a sack of bullets ; in his rifle
He poured them, and another gun like charged
Left for the Bustard.

   Now arrived more *Jägers.*
Confused they grow, together crowded, stumbling ;
The nobles cannot in the tumult smite
With cross-cut, and the *Jägers* cannot fire.
Now hand to hand they fight, steel, tooth by tooth,
Encountering steel, is shivered ; bayonet
Meets sabre, scythe on hilt is broken, fist
Meets fist, and arm meets arm.   But Rykow hastes
With some part of the *Jägers,* where the barn

Doth meet the hedge ; there stands he, to his
    soldiers
He calls, to end a battle so misruled,
Wherein, with weapons never used, they fall
Beneath the blows of fists.   Enraged that he
Himself may fire not, since in such a crowd
He knows not Muscovites from Poles, he cries,
" Draw up ! " which meaneth, form in rank and file.
But 'mid the shouting none his orders heard.

Old Matthew, for these combats hand to hand
Unsuited, backward drew, a clear space made
To right and left before him on his way.
Here, with his sabre's end, the bayonets
He wipes off from the barrels of the guns,
As candle-wicks from lights ; then, backwards
    striking
He heweth down, or pierceth ; thus retreated
The prudent Matthew from the battlefield.

But with the greatest fury on him rushed
An old Gefreiter,* trainer to the regiment,
A mighty master of the bayonet.

---

* Germ. *Gefreiter*, a lance-corporal.

He gathered him together, bent, and seized
The carbine in both hands, the right upon
The lock, the left the barrel midmost grasped.
He twisted, skipped, at times seemed half to sit,
And with his right hand forward pushed the gun,
Like sting from snaky jaws, and once again
He drew it backwards, leaning on his knee.
Thus twisting, springing, Matthew he attacked.

Old Matthew straight discerned his foeman's skill,
And with his left hand placed his spectacles
Upon his nose, the right against his breast
Sustained the handle of the Rod ; he drew
Back, the Gefreiter's motions with his eyes
Pursuing.   He himself upon his legs
Went sloping, as though drunken.   The Gefreiter
More quickly runs, and sure of victory,
To reach the easier his retreating foe,
He rose, and all his right arm far outstretched,
The rifle forward pushing, so he made
Himself the stronger by the force of pushing,
And weapon's weight, until he forward bent.
And Matthew thither, where the bayonet
He saw inserted in the barrel, placed
His Rod beneath, and upwards smote the weapon ;

Then dropping presently his Rod, he slashed
The Russian on the hand; once, and again
With backward stroke he cleft in twain his jaw.
Thus the Gefreiter fell, chief fencing-master
Among the Muscovites, and cavalier
With crosses three, and medals four.

                               Meanwhile,
Around the stocks the nobles' left-hand wing
Already were near victory.   There fought
The Sprinkler, seen from far, the Razor moved
Among the Muscovites; one cut them through
The middle of the body, on the head
The other smote them, like to that machine
Which German masters have invented, called
A thrasher; but it is at the same time
A straw-cutter, possessing flails and knives,
It chops up straw and beats out grain at once.
Thus do the Sprinkler and the Baptist work
In common, slaying foes, one from above,
And from below the other.

                        But the Baptist
Now casts aside his certain victory.
He rushes to the left wing, where fresh danger
Is threatening Matthew.   The Gefreiter's death
Avenging, with a long spontoon comes on

An ensign.   A spontoon at once is spear
And axe, neglected, or only used
On board the fleet; but at that time it served
The infantry.   The ensign, a young man,
Moved round with skill; oft as his foeman thrust
Aside his weapon, back he drew, and Matthew
Could not the young man overtake, and thus,
Or wounding or not wounding, he must fain
Defend himself.   Now with the pike the ensign
Had given him a light wound; now on high
His battle-axe upraising, he prepared
To deal the blow.   The Baptist could not run
Up to the spot, but stood half-way and whirled
His weapon round, and underneath the feet
He threw it of the foe.   He broke a bone;
The spontoon from his hand the ensign dropped;
He tottered; on him falls the Baptist; him
A crowd of nobles follow, and upon
The nobles rush the Muscovites confused
From the left wing.   War now began around
The Sprinkler.

       For the Baptist, who in helping
Matthew had lost his sword, well-nigh had paid
This service with his own life.   For on him
There fell two powerful Russians from behind,

And all at once the fourfold hands were tangled
Among his hair; fast planted on their feet,
They pulled as tight as springy ropes, fast bound
Unto a barge's mast.   In vain the Baptist
Dealt blind strokes backwards; he was failing
    fast.
But presently he saw that near to him
Gervasy combated; he shouted loud,
" Jesus, Maria!   Penknife !"
                  By the shout
Knowing the Baptist's trouble, turned the Klucznik,
And the blade lowered of the flexile steel,
Between the Baptist's head and Russians' hands.
They drew back, uttering loudly piercing cries.
But one hand, stronger tangled in the hair,
Remained there hanging, dripping streams of
    blood.

Thus a young eagle, who has struck one claw
Into a hare to hold the quarry fast
While clinging with the other to a tree,
Struggling to liberate himself, half tears
In twain the spreading eagle; in the wood
Remains the right claw, but the left, all bleeding,
Is borne off by the hare into the plains.

The Baptist being free, turns round his eyes,
Stretches his hands, and for a weapon seeks,
Calls for a weapon.   Meanwhile with his fist
He threatens, standing strong in act to walk,
Himself protecting by Gervasy's side,
Till in the crush he views his son the Bustard.
The Bustard with his right hand points his gun,
The left behind him drags a six-foot tree,
All armed with flints, and knobs, and hardened
    knots,[5]
No hand could lift it but the Baptist's own.
Soon as his well-loved arm the Baptist viewed,
His Sprinkler, swift he seized it, kissed it, sprang
With joy; he whirled it round his head, at
    once
In blood imbrued.

            What deeds he after did,
Or what defeat around him spread, 'twere vain
To sing; for none would credit give the Muse,
As none to that poor woman credit gave,
In Wilna, who, while standing on the height
Above the Ostra gate, beheld how Dejow,
The Russian leader, with a Cossack regiment
Entering, already open forced the gate;
And now one burgher, Czarnobacki named,

Slew Dejow, and annihilated all
The Cossack regiment.[6]
     'Tis enough that thus
It happened even as Rykow had foreseen ;
The *Jägers* in the crowd succumbed unto
The strength of their antagonists.   On earth
Of slain lay twenty-three ; some thirty groaned
With wounds all covered ; many fled and hid
Within the orchard, 'mid the hops, beside
The river ; some into the house had rushed
Beneath the vantage of the women there.

With shout of joy the conquering nobles rushed—
These to the wine-casks, these to strip the spoils
From off their foes.   Robak alone did not
The triumphs of the nobles share ; though he
Himself had fought not hitherto—the canons
Forbid a priest to fight—he as a man
Of great experience gave counsels, viewed
The field of battle round from different sides ;
With glance, with beckoning of hand, he gave
Fresh courage to the combatants, and guided
Their movements.   And he now unto them called
To join themselves to him, to strike on Rykow,
To make the victory complete.   Meanwhile

He through an envoy signified to Rykow,
That if he would lay down his arms he should
Preserve his life; but if he still delay
To give his sword up, Robak will command
To hem the remnant in, and cut them down.

In no wise Captain Rykow quarter asked.
The half-battalion gathering round himself,
He cried, " Make ready ! "   Presently the file
Their rifles grasped, the weapons crashed, but they
Were loaded long before.   He cried, " Present ! "
In long file gleamed the guns ; he cried out,
      " Fire
In turn ! " one after other thundered loud.
While one takes aim, one loads, another grasps
The rifle in his hand.   Resounds the hiss
Of bullets, click of locks, the ramrod's crash ;
The whole file like a moving reptile seems,
A thousand glittering feet together moving.

'Tis true that all the *Jägers* drunken were
With the strong liquor, for they aimed but ill,
And missed ; they rarely wound, and seldom kill ;
And yet two Matthews have already wounds,
And one of the Bartholomews lies low.

The nobles rarely fire, with but few guns ;
They would with sabres strike upon the foe.
The elder men restrain them ; thick the balls
Whistle, they wound, they drive on; soon they
    make
The courtyard clear before them, now begin
To clatter on the mansion's window-panes.

Thaddeus, who by his uncle's orders had
Stayed in the mansion to defend the women,
Now hearing loud and louder rage the fight,
Ran forth; the Chamberlain rushed after him,
Since Thomas brought to him at length his sabre.
He hastened, joined him to the noblemen,
And placed him at their head; rushed on, upraised
His sword ; the nobles at his pointing moved.
The *Jägers*, them admitting, poured a hail
Of bullets. Wounded lay Isajewicz,
Wilbik, and Razor. Robak after this
Restrains the nobles on one side, and Matthew
Restrains them on the other. In their zeal
The nobles colder grow, look round, draw back.
The Russians mark this. Captain Rykow thinks
To strike the last blow, from the court to drive
The nobles, and the mansion to command.

"Form for the charge!" he cried, "and to your
    pikes.
Forward!" and presently the file, their stocks
Planting like hop-poles, bent their heads, and
    marched
Forwards, and quickened step. In vain the nobles
Resist them from the front, fire on the wings;
The file already had o'er-passed the court.
The Captain, pointing with his sword unto
The house-door, crieth, "Yield, Soplica, or
I'll give command to fire the house!" "Then
    fire it,"
Replied the Judge, "I'll fry me at that fire."

O house of Soplicowo! if unhurt
Thy white walls gleam beneath the elm-trees still;
If still the assembly of the neighbouring nobles
Sit at the Judge's hospitable board,
They surely often drink the Bucket's health;
Without him Soplicowo were undone.

The Bucket hitherto few proofs of courage
Had given, though from the stocks the first set free
Among the nobles, though immediately
He found his well-loved Bucket in the cart,

His favourite gun, there with a sack of balls.
He would not fight; he trusted not himself,
He said, while fasting.   So he went where stood
A tub of spirits, in his hand he raised
The stream, as with a spoon, unto his lips.
Then, soon as he well strengthened was and warmed,
He set his cap right; from his knees he took
The Bucket in both hands; the powder rammed
Down in the gun, and poured the priming o'er,
And looked upon the battle-field.   He saw
How that bright wave of bayonets smote and
      sundered
The nobles; he against this billow swam;
He stooped him down to earth, and dived among
The thick grass in the courtyard's midst; till there,
Where nettles grew, he close in ambush laid,
And called by signs the Bustard to him.

                       He
Stood on the threshold, with his gun defending
The mansion, for his dear Sophia lived there;
And though by her his suit remained despised,
He loved her ever, and in her defence
Were glad to perish.
              Now the file of *Jägers*
Already on the nettles had encroached

Marching, when Bucket drew the trigger back;
And from the jaws of that deep-throated gun
A dozen balls all jagged let he fly
Among the Muscovites.   A second dozen
The Bustard hurls.   The *Jägers* were confused,
And frightened at the ambush, all the file
Wound in a knot, drew back, threw out their
    wounded,
And then the Baptist drove them back again.

The barn was far off.   Fearing a long round,
Beneath the garden wall had Rykow sprung,
There in their course he stayed his flying band,
He ranked them, but he changed their form of file.
Of one file he composed a triangle,
The sharp wedge pointed forward, but two sides
He placed against the garden wall.   Well did he,
For horsemen from the castle rushed on him.

The Count, who in the castle under guard
Of Muscovites had been, when fled dispersed
The frightened guard, his courtiers placed on horse;
And hearing shots, he led his cavalry
Right under fire; himself the foremost rode,
With sabre lifted high.   Then Rykow cried,

"The half-battalion fire!"   A fiery thread
Then flew along the locks, and from the sable
Barrels projecting forward, whistled forth
Three hundred bullets.   Of the cavalry
Three fell down wounded; one man lay a corpse.
The Count's horse fell, and fell the Count; the
    Klucznik
Ran, crying out for help, for he had seen
The *Jägers* for their target take the last
Of the Horeszkos, by spindle side.
Robak stood nearer; with his body he
The Count did cover, and for him received
The shot; he drew him from beneath his horse,
Commanded that the nobles step apart,
Take better aim, and spare resultless shots,
And lurk behind the hedges, or the wells,
Behind the walls of cowsheds; and the Count
Shall with his horsemen wait a better time.

Most marvellously Thaddeus understood
The plans of Robak, and accomplished them.
He stood concealed behind a wood-built well,
And as he aimed with coolness and with skill
From a two-barrelled gun—he well could hit
A florin thrown in air—inflicted thus

Most horrid wounds on Muscovy. He chose
The seniors; and his first shot slew at once
A sergeant-major, then from both the barrels
Each after each he cut two sergeants off.
Now at the borders of the triangle
He shot, now at the midst, where stood the staff.
At this impatiently did Rykow rage,
Stamped with his feet, and gnawed his sabre's hilt.
Cried, " Major Plut, what is to come of this ?
Soon none will here remain to give commands."

So Plut in anger said to Thaddeus,
" Shame on you, Master Pole, to hide behind
A piece of wood ; be not a coward, come
Out in the midst; fight honourably, like
A soldier."   To him Thaddeus made reply,
" Then, Major, if you are so bold a knight,
Why hide you thus behind a *Jäger's* collar ?
I am not afraid of you ; come from behind
The hedges ; you have caught it on your face ;
But yet I'm ready still to fight with you.
Why all this bloodshed ? For between us two
This quarrel was ; let pistols or the sword
Decide it.   I will give you choice of arms,
From cannons down to pins. If not, I'll shoot

You all like wolves in pitfalls." Saying this,
He fired, and aimed so well, that the lieutenant
He struck who stood at side of Rykow.

                                     " Major,"

Did Rykow whisper, "go you forth to duel ;
Revenge his earlier doings in the morn :
For if another slay this nobleman,
You will not, Major, wash away your shame.
This noble must be lured into the plain.
The rifle may not slay him, but the sword.
' What knocks no art is ; I prefer what pierces,'
Did old Suwarow say ; go to the plain,
Or he will shoot us, Major, every one.
Look, now he's taking aim." Thereto the Major :
" Rykow, dear friend, a dreadful fellow thou
Art with the sword ; go thou forth, brother Rykow.
Or hark ye what, I'll send out some lieutenant ;
I as the Major may not leave the soldiers,
For I am in command of the battalion."
This hearing, Rykow raised his sword, went forth
Boldly, commanded firing to give o'er ;
Waved a white cloth, and asked of Thaddeus
What weapon pleased him. The conditions made,
They both agreed on swords. But Thaddeus
     had

No sword, and while they sought for one on rushed
The Count all armed, and broke their conference off.

He cried out, " Pan Soplica, by your leave,
You have the Major challenged.   With the captain
I have a previous quarrel.   In my castle "—
" Say, sir," broke in Protasy, " in *our* castle "—
" He entered," said the Count, concluding, " at
The head of all those thieves.   He—I knew
        Rykow—
Bound fast my jockeys.   Him I will chastise,
As I chastised the robbers 'neath that rock,
Which the Sicilians call Birbante-Rocca."

All then was silent, and the firing ceased.
Both armies gazed with curiosity
Upon the meeting of their generals.
The Count and Rykow went, they turned aside,
Each other with the right hand threatening,
And right eye ; with their left hands then they bare
Their heads, and courteously salute ; the custom
Of honour, ere it come to murdering,
First to salute.   Their swords already met,
And had begun to clash.   The heroes lift
Their feet, and on the left knee kneel, by turns
Backward and forward springing.

But as Plut
Saw Thaddeus standing right before his front,
He spoke in whispers to Gefreiter Gont,
Who passed as foremost shooter in the band.
" Gont," said the Major, " see'st that gallows-
    thief?
If thou canst lodge a bullet in him, there
Beneath the fifth rib, thou shalt get from me
Four silver roubles."   Gont turned round his gun,
Stooped to the lock, his faithful comrades with
Their mantles hid him, and he fired, not at
The rib, but at the head of Thaddeus ;
Shot, and hit very near, in middle of
The hat. Aside turned Thaddeus ; then the Baptist
On Rykow fell, and all the nobles after,
Exclaiming, "Treachery!" Him shielded Thaddeus.
Scarce Rykow in retreating could succeed,
And fall into the centre of his ranks.

Once more did the Dobrzynskis onward charge,
Vying with Litva ; spite of discord past
Between the parties, all like brothers fought,
The one cheered on the other.   The Dobrzynskis,
Who saw Podhajski wheel around before
The *Jäger* ranks, down-mowing with his scythe,

Cried out rejoicing, "The Podhajc live !
Forward, Litvini brothers ! Litva, Litva !"
The Skolubowie, seeing valiant Razor,
Though wounded, fly on with his sword raised high,
Cried out, "The Matthews ! long live the Masovians !"
Each giving heart to each, they charge upon
The Russians ; vainly Robak and Matthias
Would hold them back.

               While thus they smote the band
Of *Jägers* from the front, the Wojski left
The battle-field, and towards the garden went,
And at his side the sage Protasy came.
The Wojski gave him orders whispering.

There stood within the garden, close unto
The very wall that Rykow chose as base
For his triangle, a large ancient cheese-store,
Builded in lattices, with rafters bound
Cross-ways, in cage-like form.   Within it gleamed
Great heaps of whitest cheeses, and around
Were sheaves of herbs there laid to dry, of sage,
Of *carduus benedictus*, and wild thyme ;
A herbary complete, the Wojski's daughter's
Store of domestic medicine.   Above,
The cheese-store was some seven ells in breadth.

Below, it rested on one mighty pillar,
Like a stork's nest. That old and oaken column
Leaned sidewards, 'twas already half-decayed,
And threatened accident. Not once alone
The Judge was counselled to throw down the house,
Made weak by age; but always said the Judge,
He rather would repair than pull it down,
Or else he would rebuild. Thus he delayed
The building till some more convenient time;
Meanwhile beneath the pillar he caused place
Two props; the building thereby reinforced,
But yet unlasting, o'er the garden wall
Looked down on Captain Rykow's triangle.

Towards this cheese-house silently the Wojski
And Wozny go; each with a monstrous pole,
As with a spear is armed, the housekeeper
Hastes through the hemp-plants after them, likewise
The scullion, though a small boy, very strong.
When there, upon the rotten column's top ;
They placed the poles, and pushed with all their
       strength,
As watermen push off a barge when moored
On sandy shallows, and away from shore
With long poles push it off into the deep.

The column shook, the cheese-house tottered, fell
Headlong with crash of wood and cheeses on
The Muscovite triangle, crushing, wounding,
And slaying; where the files had stood, now lay
Corpses, and wood, and cheeses white as snow,
Defiled with blood and brains.   The triangle
Broke into fragments, and the Sprinkler thundered
Upon their midst; already gleamed the Razor,
And the Rod smote; from forth the house there
    rushed
A crowd of noblemen, and from the gates
The Count his cavalry did hurl upon
The fugitives.
          Eight *Jägers* now alone,
Their sergeant at their head, still make defence.
The Klucznik rushes up, they boldly stand,
Nine barrels pointed straightway at his head.
He rushed upon their shot, the Penknife's blade
Round whirling.   This the priest perceiving, ran
Across the Klucznik's way, himself he falls,
And strikes Gervasy's foot.   They fell, just when
The platoon fired.   The lead scarce whistled by,
When up Gervasy stood.   Into the smoke
He sprung, at once swept off two *Jagers'* heads.
The rest in terror fled; he them pursued,

And smote; they ran across the courtyard, he
Behind them.   In the barn doors opening wide
They rushed.   Gervasy rushed into the barn
Upon their necks, and vanished in the dark,
But not neglected battle.   Through the doors
Came groans, a shouting, and blows thickly dealt.
Soon all was silent.   Forth Gervasy came
With bloody sword, alone.

                    The nobles now
Had cleared the plain, pursued the *Jägers*, scattered,
Cut down, ran through.   Rykow alone remained.
He cried he never would lay down his arms,
And fought on, when the Chamberlain now came
Towards him, who with sword uplifted said,
" Captain, you will not stain your honour by
Accepting quarter; you have given proof,
Unfortunate, though brave, of courage; lay'
Your sword down, ere we with our sabres shall
Disarm you; you shall keep both life and honour.
You are my prisoner."

                    Then Rykow, by
The Chamberlain's exceeding dignity
Now vanquished, bowed low, and to him his sword,
Unsheathed, with blood-stained hilt gave up; then
    said,

"Ye Lachy! brothers! woe to me that I
Had not a single cannon.   Well Suwarow
Was used to say, 'Remember, comrade Rykow,
Without some cannon never march on Poles.'
The *Jägers* all were drunk! the Major let
Them drink!   Oh, Major Plut was very wilful.
But he shall answer to the Czar, for he
Was in command.   But I, Sir Chamberlain,
Will be your friend.   A Russian proverb says,
'Who loveth greatly, he, Sir Chamberlain,
Will stoutly fight.'   You are good at drinking-bout
And good at fighting out, but cease to vent
On *Jägers* your excesses."

                        Hearing this,
The Chamberlain his sabre straight upraised,
And through the Wozny proclamation made
Of general pardon ; then he gave command
To look unto the wounded, clear the field
Of corpses, and the disarmed *Jägers* lead
Away as prisoners.   Long they searched for Plut.
He, deeply buried in the nettles, lay
As lifeless ; but at last came forth, when he
Became aware the battle all was done.
Such ending the last foray had in Litva.[7]

NOTES TO BOOK IX.

1.   " *Though a Muscovite,*
A good man."

In this representation of a Russian officer as an honourable and just man, and one of his own countrymen as most unjust and tyrannical, our author has shown how little of a narrow or exclusive character was his patriotism.

2.   " *What is*
The Yellow Book ? " *the Judge inquired.*

* The Yellow Book, so named from its cover, is the code of the martial laws of Russia.   Sometimes in time of peace the government proclaims whole provinces in a state of war, and by authority of the Yellow Book gives to the military commander full authority over the lives and property of the inhabitants.   It is known that from the year 1812 till the revolution the whole of Lithuania was subjected to the Yellow Book, the executor whereof was the Grand Duke Constantine.

3. " *Well Baka wrote.*"

Baka, a jovial ecclesiastic in Poland of the last century ; a poetaster chiefly known by his humorous veridicisms, written in most ludicrous forms.   His verses are immortal only on account of their technical absurdities and intrinsic satire. One of them begins :

> " Babula,
>   Cebula,"

and goes on thus in single trisyllabic words or three mono-syllabic ones. It requires uncommon lucidity of mind to understand it.—E. S. N.

4. " *At welba-cwelba.*"

A corruption of the German *elf zuolf* (eleven-twelve), a game at cards.—E. S. N.

5.   " *A six-foot tree,*
All armed with flints, and knobs, and hardened knots."

* The Lithuanian clubs were made in this manner; a young oak was selected, and an incision made in it with an axe, so as to cut through the bark and marrow. In these notches were inserted sharp flints, which in time grew into the wood, and formed hard knobs. Clubs constituted in pagan times the chief weapon of the Lithuanian infantry ; they are still occasionally used, and called *nasieki.*

6. " *And how one burgher,*" &c.

* After Jasinski's insurrection, when the Lithuanian army had retired towards Warsaw, the Muscovites approached Wilna, left open to their attacks. General Dejow, at the head of his staff, entered by the Ostra Gate. The streets were empty, the inhabitants having shut themselves up in their houses. One citizen, finding a cannon abandoned in an alley, loaded with grape-shot, pointed it at the gate, and fired it off. This single shot saved Wilna for the time being.

General Dejow, with some of his officers, perished ; the rest, fearing an ambush, retired from the town. The name of the citizen is not known for certain.

7. "*Such ending the last foray had in Litva.*"

* There were, however, some forays later on, which, though not so glorious, were celebrated and bloody enough. About the year 1817 a certain U——, in the Novogrodek palatinate, slew in a foray the whole garrison in the town, and took the leaders prisoners.

BOOK X.

———◆———

EMIGRATION—JACEK.

Council concerning the safety of the victors—Conventions with Rykow—Leave-takings—Important disclosure—Hope.

THOSE morning clouds, erst scattered like black
    birds,
Soaring in heaven's highest region, now
Together gathered closer.   Scarce the sun
Had from the south descended, than their flock
Had with a mighty cloud all heaven o'erspread.
The wind with ever greater swiftness drove them ;
The cloud grew ever thicker, lower hung,
Till by one side half-severed from the sky,
Stooping towards the earth, and spread abroad
Like a great sail, all winds within itself
Gathering, it flew through heaven from south to west

Then came a while of silence, and the air
Stood dumb and silent, as though mute with fear;
The fields of corn, that first lay down on earth,
And shook again aloft their golden ears,
Like billows seething, now unmoving stood,
And gazed towards heaven, with upbristling straw;
And the green willows, and the poplars standing
Beside the ways, that first like women mourning
Beside an open grave, their foreheads smote
Upon the earth, their long arms flung abroad,
Dishevelled on the wind their silvery hair,
Now, as   though   lifeless,   with   mute   mourning
      gaze,
They stand like images of Niobe.
Alone the trembling aspen shakes grey leaves.

The cattle, used to turn home leisurely,
Now ran tumultuous, nor their guardian wait,
Abandoning their pasture, home they fly.
The bull the earth upturneth with his hoof,
Ploughs with his horn, and terrifies the herd
With roar ill-boding; and the cow, who raised
Her large eyes only once unto the sky,
Her mouth in wonder opened wide, and drew
A deep sigh.   And the hog behind did linger,

Dashed round, and gnashed his teeth, and from
    the corn
Abstracted portions, and them snatched as food.
The birds lay hidden in the woods, beneath
The thatch, and in deep places of the grass.
The rooks alone in troops surround the ponds,
And walk about with slow and solemn steps,
Turning their black eyes to the clouds as black,
Their tongues forth putting from their dry, wide
    throats,
And, spreading wide their wings, await their bath.
Last of the birds, unreachable in flight,
A daring swallow, like an arrow through
The dark cloud pierces, then like bullet falls.

The nobles in that very moment ended
That horrid battle with the Muscovites,
And sought for shelter in the house and barns.
They leave the field of battle, where full soon
The elements in battle join.
               Towards
The west, still golden, shone with gloomy gleam,
The earth, a yellow red. The cloud already
Its shades outspreading, like a net in form,—
Did apprehend the remnants of the light,

And flew behind the sun, as though to seize him
Before the west. Some few storms whistled through
The air below, one after other flying,
And casting drops of rain, great, bright, and round,
As grain-like hail.

     The storm-winds suddenly
Grappled together, broke in twain; they struggled,
And whirled in whistling circles o'er the ponds,
Troubling their waters to their very depth.
They fell upon the meadows, whistling loud
Through osiers and through grass; the osier boughs
Asunder crack, and blades of grass fly wide
Upon the winds, like handfuls of torn hair,
Mixed with the ringlets of the corn-sheaves. Loud
The winds did howl, fell on the plain, contended,
Roared, tore up furrows; made an opening for
A third, which from the field itself up-tore
Like column from the dark earth, rose up, rolled
Round like a moving pyramid; its head
Deep burrowed in the ground, and from its feet
Cast sand in the stars' eyes; at every step
It swelled out broadly, shot up tall aloft,
And blew a storm upon its mighty trumpet,
Till in this chaos of water and of dust,
Of straws, and leaves and branches, torn-up turf,

The storms upon the forest smote, and roared
Within its deepest wilderness like bears.

But now as from a sieve plashed down the rain,
Unceasing, in thick falling drops.   And then
The thunders roared, the drops together ran.
Now like straight cords with tresses long they
    bind
The heavens to the earth.   Now forth they burst,
As from a pail in watery strata.   Now
Both heaven and earth are totally concealed;
Night darkens them, with storm more dark than
    night.
At times the horizon bursts from end to end,
And the storm-angel, like a mighty sun,
Unveils the lightnings of his countenance,
And, covered with a pall, retires again
In heaven, and shuts its doors with thunder noise.
Again the storm gains strength, tempestuous rain,
A heavy darkness, thick, nigh tangible;
Once more a stiller rain doth murmur, sleeps
The thunder for a moment; once more wakes,
It roareth loud, and waters plash, till all
Is peaceful.   Only trees around the house
Rustled, and rain was softly murmuring.

On such a day, the fiercest storm was welcome ;
Because the tempest, covering o'er the field
With twilight, deluged all the roads, and broke
The bridge that spanned the river ; of the farm
A fortress inaccessible it made.
So that which happened in Soplica's camp,
To-day no rumour through the neighbourhood
Could circulate ; and at the present time
The nobles' fate upon a secret hung. ,

Counsels of weight pend in the Judge's room.
The Bernardine lay wearied on the bed,
Pale, stained with blood, but wholly sound in mind.
He gives commands, the Judge exact fulfils ;
Entreats the presence of the Chamberlain,
Summons the Klucznik, Rykow there to bring
Commands.   The door then closes.   One whole
      hour
These secret conversations lasted, till
With these words Captain Rykow broke them off,
A bag with ducats heavy throwing down—
" Ye Polish sirs, among you is a saying,
That every Muscovite's a thief.   Say ye,
Whoever asks, you know a Muscovite,
Named Nikita Nikiticz Rykow, captain

Of a band, who gained eight medals and three
    crosses—
I pray you to remember that—this medal
At Oczakow, this one at Ismail,
This for the fight at Novi, and this one
At Preussisch-Eylau, this at Korsakow's
Famous retreat from Zurich,[1] and I gained
Likewise a sword for courage shown, likewise
Three testimonials of his satisfaction
From the Field-Marshal, by the Emperor
Three times commended, four times mentioned, all
In writing "——

        " But, but, Captain," Robak spoke,
" Whatever will become of us, if you
Wilt not be reconciled?   Indeed, you have
Given us your word to simplify this thing."

" True, and I pledge my word to you again,'
Says Rykow; "here's my word! What good would
    ´ come
Of ruining you?   I am an honest man.
I love you, Lachy, gentlemen, for you
Are merry folk, good at a drinking-bout,
And gallant folk too, good at fighting out.
We have a Russian proverb, ' He who rides

Upon the waggon, oft is used to be
Under the waggon;' 'Who to-day is foremost
To-morrow's in the rear;' 'To-day thou beatest,
To-morrow thou art beaten.'   Is that cause
For anger?   That is how we soldiers live.
Why such great malice should a man conceive,
Or angry be at losing?   All that work
At Oczakow was bloody, and at Zurich
They slew our infantry; at Austerlitz
I lost my whole band; but before that time,
Did your Kosciuszko at Raclawice [2]
(Where I was sergeant) mow down my platoon,
With scythes.   But what of that?   Then I again,
At Maciejowice,[3] slew with mine own hand
Two valiant nobles; one was Mokronowski.
He with his scythe had come before our front,
And cut off from a cannonier his hand,
Grasping the match.   Oh! oh! ye Lachy! Country!
I feel all that.   I, Rykow—Still the Czar
Commands this, but I pity you.   What should
The Lachy be to us?   For Muscovites
Muscovia; Poland for the Poles;—but then—
The Czar will not allow it!"
                              Unto him
The Judge replies: "Sir Captain, that thou art

An honest man, the country-folks have seen
'Mid whom so many years you have been quartered.
Be you not angry at this gift, good friend ;
We would not work you wrong ; these ducats here
We ventured to subscribe, as knowing you
Art not a rich man."

          " Ah ! the *Jägers*," cried
Rykow; "the whole band run through ! my
    division !
And all that Plut's fault.   He was in command,
And he must answer to the Czar for this.
But you take back your money, gentlemen ;
I have indeed but wretched captain's pay,
But 'tis enough to give me punch and pipe.
But you I like, since I have drunk with you,
And eaten.   I'll be merry, chatter, and
Thus will I live.   But I'll be your defence ;
And as there will be inquest, on my word
Of honour, I will give my witness for you,
That we came here upon a visit, drank,
And danced together, somewhat tipsy got,
And Plut by chance commandment gave to fire,
And so we fought, and wasted the battalion.
You, sirs, grease the Commission well with gold ;
'Twill soon despatch.   But now I'll tell you this,

Which to this nobleman I said before,
Who wears the lengthy rapier; in command
Plut was the first, I second; Plut remains
Alive, perhaps he'll bend you such a hook,
That you will perish, he's a cunning blade.
You must with bank-notes gag him. Well then, now,
Sir noble, thou with the long rapier, hast thou
Seen Plut already, taken counsel with him?"

Gervasy looked round, and his bald crown stroked,
And with a careless gesture waved his hand,
As by this sign he gave to them to know
That he had made all easy. Rykow still
Insisted. "What, will Plut be silent? has he
Then given his word?" The Klucznik, vexed that
      Rykow
Tormented him with questions, bent his finger
To earth most solemnly, then waved his hand,
As though he cut all further talk in twain,
And said, "I by the Penknife swear that Plut
Will let out nothing. He will nevermore
Converse with any one." Then dropped his hand,
And snapt his fingers, as though shaking out
Some secret from his hands.

                    This darkling gesture

The hearers comprehended, and they stood
With wonder looking on each other, still
Inquiring of this thing.   Some minutes yet
A gloomy silence lasted, till at last
Said Rykow, "Long the wolf has borne away,
Now is the wolf borne off!"*   The Chamberlain
"*Requiescat in pace*" added.   "Even in this,
Was," said the Judge, "the finger of the Lord!
But I am guiltless of this blood, I knew
Not of it."
                    From the pillow started up
The priest, and upright sat with gloomy cheer.
"Great sin an unarmed captive 'twas to slay!
Christ forbids vengeance even on a foe.
Fie! Klucznik! thou shalt answer heavily
For this before the Lord.   One reservation
Alone there is, if this committed were
Not for mere foolish vengeance, but instead,
Pro bono publico."   The Klucznik nodded,
And waved his hand extended; murmuringly
Repeated he, "*Pro bono publico.*"

And no one after spoke of Major Plut;

---

* "*Nosil wilk, poniesli i wilka.*"   A proverb.

They sought him vainly on the morrow, in
The mansion, vainly for the corpse proclaimed
Reward; the Major without trace was gone,
As he had fallen in the water. What
Had come of him, were different stories told;
But none for certain knew nor then, nor after.
In vain with questionings did they torment
The Klucznik; nought he said, except these words,
" *Pro bono publico.*" The Wojski was
Within the secret, but as he was bound
By word of honour, the old man was silent,
As though enchanted.

           After the conclusion
Of these conditions, Rykow left the room,
But Robak all the warrior noblemen
Commanded thither; and the Chamberlain
Addressed them thus with great solemnity:
" Brothers, the Lord has blessed our swords to-day.
But without reservation, I to you
Must give to know that ill effects will come
From these unhappy wars. We all have erred,
And none of us here is without his fault;
Friar Robak, that he spread too busily
The news abroad, the Klucznik and the nobles
That they misunderstood it. War with Russia

Cannot so quickly be begun.   Meanwhile
Who in the battle took most active part,
Cannot with safety tarry here in Litva,
So must ye quickly to the Duchy fly.
Matthew especially, the Baptist called,
Thaddeus and Razor, and the Bucket, bear
Their heads beyond the Niemen, where await them
Our national hosts.   We on you absent ones
Will lay the blame entirely, so shall we
Preserve the rest of all the family.
I bid ye farewell not for long.   There are
Most certain hopes that on us with the spring
Shall brighten Freedom's dawn, and Litva, who
Now bids farewell to you as exiles, soon
Shall view you her triumphant rescuers.
All necessaries for the road the Judge
Will furnish, and myself I will assist you
With money, as I can."
                            The nobles felt
The Chamberlain had wisely counselled them ;
For well 'tis known that he who once has had
A difference with the Russian Czar, can ne'er
Be truly reconciled to him on earth ;
And either he must fight, or perish in
Siberia.   Therefore without speaking they

Gazed sadly on each other, sighed, but as
A signing of consent they bowed their heads.

The Pole, although among the nations famed
For love of native land exceeding life,
Is ready aye to leave it, and depart
Into the world's wide country, and to live
Long years in poverty and in contempt,
Battling with men and destiny, while still
This hope before him glimmers through the storm,
That yet he serves his Fatherland.
                                    They all
Declared that they were ready to set out
At once ; alone this pleased not Master Buchman.
Buchman, a prudent man, had mixed not in
The battle, but on hearing that they took
Counsel together, he made haste to give
His own opinion.   He approved the project,
But wished it were completely otherwise.
He would develop it more fully, would
Have it explained more clearly ; first appoint
Commission legally, that should consider
The emigration's aims, and means, and action ;
And many other things consider too.
Unhappily the shortness of the time

Prevented justice being done to Buchman's
Advice.   The nobles hastily took leave,
And were already starting.

                     But the Judge
Stayed Thaddeus in the room, and to the priest
Said, " Now 'tis time that I should tell to thee,
That which since yesterday I learned for certain,
Our Thaddeus loves Sophia truly.   Let him,
Before departing, for her hand entreat her.
I spoke to Telimena, she will not
Be hindrance to us ; likewise is Sophia
Conformable unto her guardians' will.
If we may not in wreath of marriage join
To-day the couple, they at least to-day,
Brother, may be affianced, ere he part ;
Since for young hearts and travellers, thou well
       knowest
What various temptations rise.   But when
The youth shall cast his eyes upon the ring,
Remembering he already is a husband,
At once the fever of temptations strange
Is cool within him ; the betrothal ring,
Believe me, has great power.

                     " Myself, I had,
Some thirty years ago, a great affection

For the fair Martha, and her heart I won.
We were betrothed, but Heaven did not bless
Our union, and soon left me desolate,
Taking the lovely Wojszczanka to
His glory, daughter of my friend Hreczecha.
As memory of her virtues, of her charms,
This gold betrothal ring alone remained
To me.   As often as I looked thereon,
My dead love stood before my eyes, and thus
By Heaven's grace I hitherto have kept
My faith to my betrothed one, and though ne'er
A husband, I am an old widower.
Although the Wojski has another daughter,
Pretty enough, and like enough unto
My well-loved Martha."

                   Saying this he looked
Upon the ring with tenderness, and brushed
A tear off with his hand; then ended: "Brother,
What thinkest thou, shall we betroth the two?
He loves, and I have the aunt's word and the girl's."

But up rushed Thaddeus, and earnestly
Spoke thus: "How can I show my gratitude
To my dear uncle, who so constantly
Thinks of my happiness!   Ah! dearest uncle,

I were the happiest of men, if now
Sophia were betrothed to me, if I
Could know she was my future wife ; and yet—
I'll say it openly—to-day these spousals
May not be done, for this are many reasons.
Ask me no more.   If Sophia deigns to wait,
She maybe will behold me better, worthier.
Maybe by steadfastness I shall deserve
Her love ; maybe a little glory may
Adorn my name.   Maybe we shall return
Soon to our native region.   Then, my uncle,
I shall recall your promise to you, then
Upon my knees salute my dear Sophia,
And if she still be free, entreat her hand.
Now must I part from Litva, it may be
For long, perhaps another may meanwhile
Commend him to Sophia.   I will not
Constrain her will, to beg return of love
Which I have not deserved, were mean and base."

And as the young lad spoke thus feelingly,
Like two great pearl-drops glittered two bright tears
Within his large blue eyes, and ran together
Swift down his blushing countenance.

                                        But curious,

Sophia from the depths of the alcove
Had heard this secret discourse, and she heard
While Thaddeus simply thus and boldly spake
His love; the heart within her trembled; she
Saw only those two large tears in his eyes;
Although she might not track his secret's thread,
Wherefore he loved her, why abandoned her,
Or whither he departed, yet this parting
Much saddened her.   The first time in her life
She from a young man's lips had heard the great
And wondrous tidings that she was beloved.
So ran she to a little household shrine,
Therefrom an image and a reliquary
She took; the picture was St. Genevieve,
And in the reliquary was a shred
Of holy Joseph's coat, the lover, patron
Of youth betrothed; and with these holy things
She entered the apartment.

                    "Are you going
So quickly?   I will give you for the journey
A little present, and a warning too.
Carry this relic with you always, and
This picture, and remember still Sophia.
May the Lord God in health and weal conduct you,
And quickly bring you back to us in joy!"

Silent she stood, and drooped her head, while half
Closed her blue eyes, and liberal tears ran forth
From underneath the lashes ; and Sophia,
Standing with eyelids closed, kept silence still,
Pouring down tears like diamonds.

      Thaddeus, taking
The gifts, and on her hand a kiss imprinting,
Said, "Lady, I must bid farewell to you.
Farewell, remember me, and deign at times
To say a prayer for me, Sophia !"   More
He could not say.

     But unexpectedly
The Count and Telimena coming in,
Observed the youthful lovers' tender parting.
The Count, much moved, at Telimena looked,
And said, " What beauty even in a scene
So simple ! when a shepherdess's soul
Must with a warrior's part, even as a boat
Parts from a ship in tempest !   Truly, nought
Can kindle tenderness within the heart,
As when heart parts from heart.   Time 'is like
  wind,
It but extinguishes a feeble light ;
A great fire flames but stronger from the wind.
My heart can love more strongly from afar.

Soplica, I have held thee for a rival,
And this mistake of our sad variance,
Which forced me to draw sword on you, one cause
Has been.   I see my error, since thou for
The shepherdess didst sigh, but I had given
My heart to this fair nymph.   Let our offences
Be drowned in blood of foes.   We will not strive
With murderers' swords against each others' lives.
Let otherwise our lovers' quarrel be
Decided ; let us strive who shall excel
In strength of love !   Let us both leave behind
The objects dear unto our hearts, and let us
Both hasten upon swords, on spears to rush.
Let us together strive in steadfastness,
In woe, in sufferings, and with valiant arm
Pursue our foes."   He spoke, on Telimena
He looked, but she replied not, sore amazed.

" But, Count," the Judge broke in, " wherefore
      must you
Depart, of such necessity ?   Believe me,
You may in safety dwell upon your lands ;
The government may strip and scourge the poor
Nobility, but you are certain, Count,
Whole to remain.   You know how high your rank ;

You are tolerably rich ; with half your income
You may redeem yourself from prison."

"That,"
The Count replied, "agrees not with my mood ;
As I may be no lover, I will be
A hero.   For the cares of love I summon
The comforters of glory ; if I am
A beggar of the heart, I will be great
In arms !"

Said Telimena : " What debars you
From love and happiness ?"   " My destiny's
Power," said the Count ; "the darkness of fore-
    bodings,
That by mysterious movement swiftly rush
To foreign regions, unaccustomed deeds.
I own I wished in Telimena's honour
To light the flame to-day at Hymen's altar,
But an example far too beautiful
This young man gives me, of his own free will
Tearing his nuptial garland off, and rushing
To prove his heart in accidents of fate,
Changing, and in the bloody chance of war.
To-day for me likewise an epoch new
Is opening.   The sounding of my sword
Birbante-Rocca once did echo back.

Oh, may its sound through Poland spread as well!"
He ended, on his sword-hilt proudly smote.

"Ay!" Robak spoke; "such good-will hard it were
To blame.   Ride off, and money take with thee.
Thou mayest perhaps equip a band of men
Like Wladimir Potocki, who amazed
The Frenchmen, giving to the treasury
A million; like Prince Dominic Radziwill,
Who pledged his lands and furniture, and armed
Two regiments of horse.   Ride off, and take
Money; we now enough of hands possess,
But there is want of money in the Duchy,
Ride ye away, we take our leave of you."

With sad eyes Telimena on him glanced.
"Alas!" she said, "I see nought will restrain thee.
My hero! when thou enterest warlike lists
On thy love's colour turn a tender glance."
Thus saying, a ribbon from her dress she took,
She fashioned therewith a cockade, and pinned it
To the Count's bosom.   "Let this colour lead thee
Up to the fiery cannon, shining spears,
And rain of bullets; when by valiant deeds
Thou winnest glory, and with deathless laurels

Thou shalt enwreathe thy blood-stained helm and
    crest
With victory proud, ev'n then turn thou thine eyes
On this cockade. Remember thou whose hand
Fastened that colour there." She reached her hand
To him. The Count then, kneeling, kissed that
    hand,
And Telimena to one eye approached
Her handkerchief, but with the other looked
From high upon the Count, who bade farewell,
Most deeply moved. She sighed—but—shrugged
    her shoulders.

But said the Judge, " Sir Count, make haste, 'tis
    late ; "
And Friar Robak cried, with threatening mien,
" Enough of this ! make haste ! " The orders thus
Both of the Judge and of the priest divide
The loving pair, and drive them from the room.

Meantime did Thaddeus embrace his uncle
With tears, and Robak's hand kissed. Robak
    pressed
Unto his bosom the lad's forehead, laying
His hands in form of cross upon his head,

Looked up to heaven, and said, "My son ! depart
With God !" and wept.   But Thaddeus already
Had passed the threshold.   " What !" then asked
   the Judge,
" Will you not tell him, brother, anything ?
And now, poor boy, shall he learn nothing, ere
He part?"—"No, nothing," said the priest, long
   weeping,
With face hid in his hands.   " And wherefore should
The poor lad know that he a father has,
Who hid him from the world, as being a villain
And murderer?   God knows, how I did long
To tell my son, but of this consolation
I make unto the Lord a sacrifice
To expiate my former crimes."

                        " Then," said
The Judge, " 'tis time to think now of thyself.
Consider at thine age, and in thy plight,
Thou couldst not with the others emigrate.
Thou once did say thou knewest a house, where
   thou
Couldst hide thyself.   Say where?   Let us make
   haste.
A carriage waiteth ready harnessed.   Was it
Not in the forest, in the keeper's hut ?"

Shaking his head, said Robak, "'Twill be time
To-morrow.   Now, my brother, send thou to
The parish priest, that he may swiftly come
Here with the sacrament.   Send all from hence ;
Thou only, with the Klucznik, here remain.
Close thou the doors."

            Robak's commands the Judge
Fulfilled, and sat beside him on the couch;
Gervasy stood, and with his elbow leaned
Upon his rapier's hilt, and with his brow
Supported on his hand.

              Robak, before
He spoke, his glance fixed on the Klucznik's face,
And kept mysterious silence.   As a surgeon
On a diseasèd body lightly lays
At first his hand, ere he the sharp blade prove,
Thus Robak softened of his piercing eyes
The glance severe ; long o'er Gervasy's face
He held them mute.   At length, as he would give
Blindfold the stroke, he covered with his hand
His eyes, and with a powerful voice he said :
" I am Jacek Soplica."

              At these words
Pale grew the Klucznik, forward bent, and stood
One half all stooping forward ; stood, supported

On one foot, like a flying stone, from high
Arrested on its path ; his eyes wide staring ;
Lips wide apart, with white teeth threatening ;
His whiskers bristling ; from his hand the rapier
Abandoned on the ground his knees held fast ;
His right hand, closely pressing, grasped the hilt.
The rapier from behind stretched after him,
Waved its long black extremity around,
Unto each side.   And like a wounded lynx
The Klucznik seemed, that from a tree will spring
Into the hunter's eyes; it puffs itself
Up in a ball; it growls, its bloodshot eyes
In sparkles kindles, moves its whiskers, lashes
Its tail.

   " Rembajlo," said the friar, " no more
The wrath of man affrights me, for I am
Already under God's hand.   I conjure
Thee in the name of Him who saved the world,
And on the cross did bless His murderers,
And did accept the thief's entreaty, that
Thou wilt be pacified, and all that I
Shall say wilt listen patiently.   I have
Confessed now whom I am, and for relief
Of conscience I must seek, and must at least
For pardon pray.   Thou listen my confession ;

Then after do thou what thou wilt with me."
And here his hands he folded, as in prayer.
The Klucznik, deep in thought, moved backward,
　　smote
His forehead, and his shoulders moved.
　　　　　　　　　　　　　The priest
Began the story to relate of his
Familiar friendship with Horeszko, how
He loved his daughter; from this cause proceeded
His quarrel with the Pantler.　But he spoke
With little order, mingling oft complaints
And lamentations in his story; often
His speech broke off, as though he had ended it.
And then again began.
　　　　　　　　　The Klucznik, knowing
Most perfectly the annals of Horeszko,
Though tangled in disorder all this tale,
In memory could range, and fill it out;
But many things the Judge nought understood.
Both listened diligently, with bowed heads,
And Jacek ever spoke with freer words,
And oft broke off.*

---

* In translating the whole of this scene, an effort has been
made to reproduce the effect of the broken lines in the
original.

" Indeed, thou knowest too well, Gervasy, how
The Pantler oft invited me to banquets,
And would propose my health ; not seldom cried,
Lifting his glass on high, he had no friend
Above Soplica.   How he then embraced me !
All who saw this would think he shared with me
His very soul.   A friend he ! well he knew
What at that time was passing in my soul !

" Meanwhile the neighbourhood already whispered,
And such a one said to me : ' Ah ! Soplica !
In vain wouldst thou compete, the threshold of
A dignitary is too high for Jacek
Podczaszyc' feet.'   I laughed, pretending I
Laughed at the magnates, and their daughters too,
And cared not for the aristocracy ;
That if I oft consorted with them, 'twas
From friendship ; I would only take for wife
One of my own condition.   Ne'ertheless
These jestings cut me to the quick.   Young then,
Courageous, all the world to me was open.
In this land, where, as well you know, a noble
By birth may for the throne be candidate
With highest lords—in truth Tenczynski once
Did ask a daughter of a royal house,[4]

And a king gave her to him without shame—
Were not Soplica's honours equal with
Tenczynski's, both by blood, and crest, and service
To the Republic?

　　　　　　　"Ah! how easily
A man may ruin another's happiness,
In one short moment, and may not repair it
In all a long life!　One word from the Pantler,
How happy we had been! who knows, maybe
We both had lived till now.　Maybe, even he,
Beside his darling child, his lovely Eva,
Beside his grateful son-in-law, had reached
A peaceful old age, and his grandchildren
Perhaps had rocked.　Now what has passed?　He
　　　ruined
Both of us, and himself!—That murderous deed,
And all the followings of that crime, and all
My woes and sins!—I have no right to complain,
I was his murderer!—I have no right
To make complaint!—I from my very heart
Do pardon him; but even he——

"If one time merely he had openly
Refused me!　For he well knew what we felt.
If he had not received my visitings—

Who knoweth how ?—I maybe had departed,
Been angry, railed against him, in the end
Neglected him.   But he in cunning proud
Thought of a new idea ; he made pretence
That such a thing had entered ne'er his head
That I could ever seek for such alliance.
But I was needful to him ; I had weight
Among the nobles, and the peasants all
Loved me ! As though he ne'er perceived my love,
He welcomed me as erst, insisted ev'n
That I should come more often.   And as oft
As we two were alone together, seeing
Mine eyes o'erclouded, and my breast o'ercharged,
And ready to break forth, the old man, cunning,
Would presently throw out indifferent words
Of lawsuits, diets, hunts——

" Ah ! o'er our cups, not seldom, when he thus
Would melt, when thus he pressed me, and assured
Me of his friendship, having need of my
Sabre, or vote in Diet—when I must
Press him in turn affectionately, then
Such anger boiled in me, that I turned o'er
The spittle in my mouth, and then my hand
Would grasp my sabre's hilt ;—I longed to spit

Upon this friendship, and to draw my sword.
But Eva, looking on my glance and posture,
Could guess, I know not how, what in me passed.
She gazed imploringly, her cheeks grew pale ;
And such a lovely dove, so gentle she—
And such a sweet look had she—so serene !
So angel-like ! I know not even how,
I had no heart to anger her, to grieve her ;
And I was silent !—I, the brawler famous
Throughout all Litva !—I, who lived no day
Without a fight, who never would submit
To wrong, not merely at the Pantler's hands,
But even at the king's ; whom slightest cross
Drove into madness.   I, though evil-minded
And drunken, was as dumb as a young lamb,
As though I saw the Holiest——

" How many times I longed to ope my heart,
And even to prayer before him humble me !
But gazing in his eyes I met a look
Cold as a stone.   Ashamed of my emotion
I was ; I hastened once again, quite coldly
Of lawsuits, diets, to discourse, and even
To jest !   True, all from pride, not to debase
The name of the Soplicas, not degrade

Myself before a lord by useless prayers,
Nor earn refusal.   For what would be said
Among the nobles, if they knew that I
I, Jacek——

"That the Horeszkos had refused
A maiden to Soplica, and to me,
Jacek, had offered the black broth![5]

                           "At last,
Not knowing how to act, I thought to gather
A slender regiment of the nobles, and
To leave for aye the district and my country ;
Somewhere in Muscovy or Tartary
To go, and war begin.   I rode to take
Leave of the Pantler, in the hope that when
He saw his staunch supporter, his old friend,
Almost an inmate of his house, with whom
He had drunken, and made war through all those
      years,
Now bidding farewell, and into the world
Riding afar, the old man might be moved,
And show me somewhat yet of human soul,
As a snail his horns——

"Ah ! who, though but in his inmost heart's depth,

Has but one spark of feeling for a friend,
But will this sparkle show on taking leave,
Having his forehead for the last time touched,
The coldest eye will often shed a tear.

"The poor girl, hearing I should go away,
Grew pale, unconscious, fell almost a corpse;
Nought could she say, until she poured a stream
Of tears! I saw how dear I was to her!
I recollect, the first time in my life,
I burst in tears of joy and of despair.
I longed again before her father's feet
To fall, to wind like serpent round his knees,
Crying, ' Dear father, take me for thy son,
Or slay me ! '—Then the Pantler, solemnly,
Cold as a pillar of salt, polite, unmoved,
Began to speak; of what?—his daughter's wedding!
That moment !—Thou, Gervasy, friend, consider;
Thou hast a human heart !

                         "The Pantler said,
' Soplica, unto me the Castellan
Has sent betrothers; thou my friend art, what
Sayest thou to this ? Thou knowest that I have
A daughter fair and rich. The Castellan
Is of Witepsk. True, in the Senate he has

A low seat, unconfirmed.   What counsel you,
Brother?'   I cannot now at all remember
What unto him I answered ; possibly
Nothing.   To horse I mounted, and I fled."

" Jacek," the Klucznik said, " excuses wise
Thou urgest, yet they lessen not thy fault.
For truly not once only in the world,
It has occurred that one who loved a daughter
Of lord or king, has tried by violent means
To win her, thought of stealing her away ;
Revenged him openly.   But thus treacherous
Death to inflict, upon a Polish lord,
In Poland, and in concert thus with Russians ! "

" No, not in concert," Jacek said in grief.
" Carry her off by violence ?   True, I could
Have done so, could have snatched her from
        behind
Gratings and latches ; could have ground to dust
That castle of his ; I had at my back
Dobrzyn and four stout clans more.   Ah ! if she
Had been as our own noble ladies, strong
And healthy ; had she feared not flight, pursuit ;
And could she but have heard the clash of arms !

But she, poor girl! so carefully her parents
Had cherished her, that she was timid, weak,
A caterpillar, a spring butterfly;
And thus to seize her, with an armèd hand
To touch her, were to slay her! No! I could
　　not!—
Revenge me openly, by storm to hurl
His castle into ruins? Shame! for men
Would say that I revenged me for refusal!
Klucznik, thine honest heart can never feel
What hell there lieth in offended pride.

" Pride's demon counselled me to better plans;
To take a bloody vengeance, but conceal
The cause of vengeance; not to visit more
The castle, root that love from out my heart;
To forget Eva, marry with another;
And then to find out later some pretext,
Revenge myself——

"Then seemed it to me, that my heart had
　　changed,
And pleased I was with this imagining,
And—married me unto the first I met,
A poor girl! Evil did I—how I was

Cruelly punished! For I loved her not,
The hapless mother of my Thaddeus!—
To me the most attached, most loving soul!—
But I within my heart my former love
And malice strangled. And I was as mad.
In vain I forced myself to husbandry,
Or business, all in vain! For by a demon
Of vengeance driven wild, bad, irritable,
I found no comforting in aught on earth.
And thus I fell from sin to other sins,
Began to drink.

"And so my wife ere long of sorrow died,
Leaving that child; but me despair consumed.

"How dear I must have held my perished love!
So many years! where have I not been? and
I cannot yet forget her, and for aye
Her loved form stands before my eyes, as painted.
I drank; I could not for a moment drink
Mem'ry away, nor of it rid myself,
Though I have traversed o'er so many lands;
And now behold, in habit of a monk,
I am God's servant, on this couch, in blood—
So long I have spoken of her!—in this moment
To speak of such things! God will pardon me!

You here must know in what despair and grief
That crime was done.

"'Twas shortly after her betrothal day;
They talked of this betrothal everywhere.
'Twas said, when Eva from the Wojewode's hand
Received the nuptial ring, she swooned, she fell
Into a fever, that she had the symptoms
Of a consumption, that she ceaseless sobbed.
'Twas guessed she loved another secretly.
But still the Pantler, ever tranquil, merry,
Gave in the castle balls, and gathered friends.
Me he invited not; in what could I
Be useful to him?   My misrule at home,
And wretchedness, my shameful custom, made
Me as a scorn and laughter to the world;—
Who once, I well may say it, shook the whole
District; whom Radziwill * belovèd called;
Who, when I forth from out my farmstead rode,
Went with a court more numerous than a prince;
And when I drew my sword some thousand sabres
Around were gleaming, frightening lordly castles.
But now the peasant children laughed at me.

---

* Prince Charles Radziwill, surnamed *Kochanck* or Beloved, from his invariable habit of thus addressing all persons.

Thus sudden grew I vile in eyes of men !
Jacek Soplica ! Who knows what is pride?"

Here feeble grew the Bernardine, and fell
Back on the couch. Then spoke the Klucznik,
   roused :

" Great are Heaven's judgments. True, true ! so
   'tis thou !
And thou art Jacek ! Thou Soplica ! under
A hood ! thou livest.as a beggar ! Thou,
Whom I remember ruddy and in health,
A handsome noble, when the ladies praised thee,
When women raved about thee ! Whisker-bearer !
Not as thou wert in former days ! thus hast thou
Grown old from sorrow ! How did I not know thee
After that shot, when thou didst hit the bear
So perfectly ? our Litva had no marksman
Surpassing thee ; thou also, after Matthew,
Wert with the sabre first ! True, in past times
Our noble ladies sang concerning thee,
' Lo ! Jacek twirls his whisker, all the regions
   shake,
And he for whom the whisker shall this twirling
   make,

Were he even Prince Radziwill, shall tremble for
    its sake.'
And thou didst twirl it even for my lord !
Unhappy one ! 'Tis thou ! brought to what state !
Jacek the Whiskered is a begging friar !
Great are Heaven's judgments ! And now, ha ! ha !
    scatheless
Thou never shall come forth ! I swear it, thou
Who hast sucked Horeszko's drops of blood away."

Meanwhile the priest sat up upon the couch,
And ended thus : " I rode around the castle.
How many devils were there in my head,
And in my heart ! who shall repeat their names ?
' The Pantler slayeth his own child. Already
Me has he slain, annihilated.' Under
The door I rode ; some devil lured me there.
Look on his riot ! Drunkenness each day
Within the castle, and how many lights
The windows show ; what music in the halls !
And will that castle not in ruins fall
Upon his bald head ?

                " Think of vengeance, swift
Will Satan give a weapon to thy hand.
Scarce I imagined it, when Satan sent

The Muscovites !   I stood on gazing.   Thou
Knowest how they stormed your castle.
                                        " But 'tis false
That I was in accord with Muscovites !

" I gazed on.   Various thoughts swarmed through
    my head.
First with a foolish smile, as children look
On conflagration, gazed I ; then I felt
A murderer's joy, and while I waited, swift
The castle walls began to burn and fall.
At times the thought possessed me to rush in,
To rescue her, the Pantler even——

" Ye did defend yourselves, thou knowest, bravely
And prudently.   I marvelled.   Round me fell
The Muscovites.   Those cattle ! ill they aim !
On viewing their disasters, once again
Did spite possess me.   Shall this Pantler be
Victorious, and shall all things in the world
Thus prosper for him ?   And shall he come forth
With triumph from this terrible attack ?
I rode away in shame.   Just then 'twas morn.
Then looked I up, I knew him.   He came forth
Upon the balcony, his diamond clasp

Did in the sunlight glitter, and he twirled
His whisker proudly, and a proud glance threw.
It seemed that unto me especially
He bade defiance, that he knew me, and
Thus stretched his hand towards me, mocking me,
And threatening.   I a Russian's rifle grasped,
Scarce pointed, scarce took aim, but off it went!
Thou knowest!——

" Cursed be those fire-arms !   He who slays with
        sword
Must place himself, attack and parry, turn ;
He may disarm his foe, may stay the sword
Half-way; but with these fire-arms ! 'tis enough
To touch the lock ! a moment ? one sole spark !

" Did I fly then, when thou took'st aim at me
From overhead ?   I fixed my eyes upon
My gun's two barrels ; and some strange despair,
Some wondrous sorrow, fixed me to the earth.
Why then, alas ! Gervasy, why didst thou
Then miss me?   Thou hadst done me service thus!
But well it might be seen for expiation
Of sin 'twas needful "——

                    Here again he failed

For want of breath. " God knows," the Klucznik
    said,
" I truly wished to hit thee ! How much blood
By that one shot of thine hast thou poured forth !
How many miseries fell on us, and on
Thine own race, all through thy fault, Master Jacek!
But when the *Jägers* for their target took
The last of the Horeszkos, although by
The spindle side, thou didst him shield, and when
A Muscovite did fire at me, thou didst
Cast me to earth, and thus didst save us both.
If true it is thou art a cloistered priest,
Thy frock alone protects thee from the Penknife.
Farewell, no more I'll tarry on your threshold.
Let us be quits, and leave to Heaven the rest."

Jacek stretched forth his hand. Gervasy drew
Backwards. " I cannot," said he, "without shame
To my nobility, e'er touch a hand
With such a murder stained, from private vengeance,
And not *pro bono publico.*"
                But Jacek
Sank from the pillows back upon the couch,
And turned towards the Judge, and ever paler,
Asked anxiously about the parish priest ;

And to the Klucznik called, "I do beseech you,
That you remain! I presently will end.
I scarce have power sufficient."

                              "What, my brother!"
The Judge exclaimed; "thy wound is not so
      grave.
What sayest thou of the parish priest? Perhaps
It was ill dressed. I'll call the doctor here.
"Or in our store of medicines"—— The priest
Broke in: "My brother, 'twere in vain! It is
A former wound from Jena; 'twas ill-healed,
And now fresh opened; there is gangrene here.
I understand wounds. Look how black the blood,
Like pitch! What use the doctor here? but that
A vain thing is! Once only can we die;
Give up our soul to-morrow, or to-day.
Sir Klucznik, wilt thou pardon me? I must
Conclude——

                  "There is in this some merit, not
To will to be a traitor to the nation,
Although the nation traitor thee proclaim;
For him, above all, in whom dwells such pride
As dwelt in me.—

                  "The name of traitor clung
To me like pestilence. All patriots

Did turn their faces from me ; former friends
Fled from me ; he who timid was, afar
Saluted and avoided me ; and even
Each wretched peasant, miserable Jew,
Although he bowed, did pierce me from aside
With mocking smile.   The name of traitor rung
Within my ears, with echo did resound
At home, abroad.   That word from morn till dusk
Before me circled, as a spot before
An eye diseased.   And yet no traitor was I
Unto my country "——

" The Muscovites would gain me partisan ;
They gave to the Soplicas a large share
Of the deceased man's lands ; and later on
The Targowica traitors [6] wished to honour
Me with an office.   If I then had willed
To Russianise myself, which Satan counselled,
I had by now most rich and powerful grown.
Had I become a Muscovite, the highest
Magnates had sought my favour, even my brother
Nobles, and even the commonality,
Who do so readily despise their own,
Forgive those happier who serve Muscovy !
I knew all that—but yet—I could not !——

" From the land I fled—
Where have I not been ? what have I not suffered?

" Until God deigned reveal the only cure :
I must reform myself, and must repair,
As far as in my power might lie——

" The Pantler's daughter, with the Wojewode,
Her husband, somewhere in Siberia
Transported, there died early.   In this country
She left Sophia, her little daughter.   I
Commanded she should be adopted——

" Maybe from foolish pride, far more than love,
I slew ; so must I show humility.
I went among the monks.   I, once so proud
Of race, I, who was as a blusterer,
Did   bow   my   head,   a   friar ;   I   called   me
      Robak,
Since like a worm in dust——

" That ill example for the Fatherland,
Encouragement to treason, it was needful
By good example to redeem, by blood,
By sacrifice——

"I for my country fought ;—but where—I say not.
'Twas not for earthly glory that I rushed
So oft on swords and shot. To me more sweet
'Tis to remember, not loud, valorous deeds,
But silent actions, useful sufferings,
Which none——

"Not one time only did I penetrate
Unto my country, bearing the commands
Of generals, collecting information,
Concluding treaties. The Galicians know
This monkish hood, the Poseners know it too.
One year I laboured in a Prussian fortress ;
Three times the Muscovites did wound my
    shoulders
With sticks, once sent me to Siberia ;
The Austrians then in Spielberg buried me
To labour in their dungeons,—*carcer durum.*
The Lord by miracle delivered me,
Permitting me to die among my people,
And with the sacraments.

"Perhaps ev'n now, who knows, maybe I sinned,
Maybe beyond the generals' commands,
I hurried insurrection on. This thought,

That the Soplica house should arm the first—
My kinsmen the first Horseman should upraise
In Litva—this thought—seemeth pure——

"Thou didst desire revenge?   Behold, thou hast it!
For thou wast instrument of God's chastising;
Heaven by thy means did cut my measures through.
Thou didst the thread so many years had spun
Tangle; the great aim which consumed my life,
My latest earthly feeling in the world,
Which I had cherished as my dearest child,
Thou in its father's eyes hast slain, and I
Forgive thee!   Thou "——

                    "May Heaven forgive us both!"
The Klucznik broke in.   "If thou art about
To take the sacrament, Friar Jacek, I
Am neither Lutheran, nor schismatic.*   Who
Afflicts the dying, I know sins heavily.
I'll tell thee somewhat that will sure rejoice thee.
When my deceasèd master wounded fell,
And I bent o'er him, kneeling, and my sword
Steeped in his wound, and swore revenge,—my lord
Did shake his head, his hand stretched towards
          the gate,

---

* Of the Greek Church.

To where thou wert, and in the air he signed
The cross. He could not speak, but gave this sign
That he forgave his murderer. I this
Did understand, but I so mad with rage
Was then, I ne'er a word spoke of this cross."

The sick man's sufferings here broke off discourse,
And one long hour of silence followed then.
They wait the priest. The sound of hoofs was
    heard ;
A breathless tenant at the chamber knocked.
He bears a letter of importance, shows it
To Jacek's self. Then Jacek to his brother
Gives it, and him desires to read aloud.
The letter was from Fisher, at that time
Commanding in the staff of Poland's army, under
Prince Joseph. He announced, that in the secret
Imperial cabinet was war declared ;
The Emperor now proclaims it to the world.
The Diet is in Warsaw summoned, and
The States Confederate of Masovia have
Decreed the union of Litvania.[7]

Jacek, in hearing, spoke a silent prayer.
A sacred taper pressing to his breast,

He raised to heaven his eyes, alight with hope,
And shed a flood of last and joyful tears.
" Now, Lord," he said, " let thou thy servant part
In peace."　All knelt; just then upon the threshold
A bell did sound, a sign the parish priest
Had with the Host arrived.

　　　　　　　　Night now had fled,
And through the milky heaven did course the first
Bright, rosy sunbeams.　Through the window-panes
They fell like diamond arrows.　On the couch
They shone reflected from the sick man's head,
And dressed in gold his brow and countenance,
That like a saint he shone in fiery crown.

NOTES TO BOOK X.

1. "*At Korsakow's Famous retreat from Zurich.*"

The dates of the battles here enumerated are as follows : Oczakow, 1788; Ismail, 1790; Novi, in the plain of Marengo, where the French were defeated by the Austro-Russian army, 1799. The retreat of Suwarow's army from Zurich took place in the same year.

2. "*Your Kosciuszko at Raclawice.*"

At the battle of Raclawice, near Krakow, Kosciuszko gained a signal victory over the Austrian and Russian troops ; in a great measure by the peasant infantry armed with scythes, which he was the first to organise, and of which he there proved the efficiency.

3. "*Again at Maciejowice.*"

Maciejowice, the field where Kosciuszko was defeated and taken prisoner by the Russians on the 10th October 1794.

4. " *Tenczynski once*
Did ask a daughter of a royal house."

John Tenczynski, in the sixteenth century, gained the love of a princess of Sweden, with the approval of her brother King Eric, but being taken prisoner at sea by the Danish fleet, died in captivity, without the consummation of his wishes. This story forms the base of a novel by Niemcewicz, and there is a very pretty poem by Karpinski on the same subject.

5. " *The black broth.*"

* Black broth, served to a suitor for the hand of a lady, signified a refusal.—See Notes to Book II.

6. " *The Targowica traitors.*"

* It would appear that the Stolnik was killed about the year 1791, in the first war [followed by the Russian occupation, and subsequent insurrection].

7. " *Decreed the union of Litvania.*"

War between France and Russia was declared on the 3d August 1811.

BOOK XI.

———•———

THE YEAR 1812.

*Spring omens—Entrance of armies—Divine service—Official
rehabilitation of Jacek Soplica—The end of the lawsuit near
at hand, to be inferred from the conversation of Gervasy and
Protasy—Love-scene between the lancer and the maiden—The
dispute concerning Kusy and Sokol is decided—The guests
assemble for the banquet—Presentation of the betrothed
couples to the generals.*

THOU year! who in our country thee beheld,
The year of beauty calls thee even now,
But year of war the soldier; even yet
Our elders love to tell of thee, even now
Song dreameth of thee.   Long wert thou proclaimed
By heavenly miracle, and thee forestalled
Dumb rumours 'mid the people; all the hearts
Of the Litvini with the sun of spring
Were girdled by some strange presentiment,
As though before the ending of the world;
Some expectation full of joy and fear.

When first they drove the cattle forth in spring,
'Twas marked, though lean and famished, they
    did not
Rush on the winter-corn, green on the glebe;
But lay down on the mead, with heads bowęd down,
To low, or chew the cud of winter food.

The villagers, who led the plough on field,
Now scarce rejoiced as they were wont to do
At ending of long winter, for no song
They sang; they laboured idly, as they neither
Recalled the seed-time nor the harvest.   At
Each step they stayed the oxen and the ponies
In harness, and with anxious heart they gazed
Towards the western quarter, as from thence
Some miracle should be revealed, and marked
With anxious heart the homeward flying birds.

For even thus early to his native pine
The stork was flying, widely he unfurled
His white wings, early standard of the spring.
And after him in noisy regiments came
Upon the waters swallows gathering thick,
Who from the late-thawed earth collected mud
To build their houses.   And at eventide

The arriving woodcocks whispering were heard
Among the thickets, and the wild-goose flock
Murmured above the wood, and wearied fell
Down with great uproar, for a halt, and in
The sky's dark depth the cranes continual cry.
Hearing, the nightly guards inquire in fear,
Whence in the wingèd kingdom such confusion ?
What storm thus early drives the birds away ?

And now behold a newer flock, that seems
Finches and plovers, starlings, flock of shining
Crests and of standards ; brightly on the hills
They shone, and on the plains they make descent.
The cavalry !   Adornments wondrous, arms
Invisible, troop after troop ; in midst
Like melted snows, along the highways, glide
Ranks sheathed in iron, from out the woods their
        caps
Swarm blackly, and a row of bayonets gleams ;
The ant-hill's swarming infantry unnumbered.

All towards the north !   It certain might be said
That in that migratory time even men,
Following the birds, were marching to our land,
Impelled by some mysterious instinct force.

Men, horses, guns, and eagles, day and night
Flow onward ; in the sky flame here and there
Wide blazes, earth is trembling, one may hear
The thunders smite on every side.

War ! war !

In Litva there is not a foot of land
Whereto its uproar does not penetrate.
'Mid the dark forest-lands the peasant, all
Whose parents and whose ancestors have died,
Not having passed beyond the forest's bounds,—
Who understood in heaven no other cries
Than those of storm-winds, nor on earth beside
The roars of beasts ; had seen no other guests
Than fellow-foresters, now sees—in heaven
A wondrous fire-blaze glowing, in the forest
A crashing hears ; some wandering cannon-ball,
Strayed from the field of battle, seeks its way
Amid the forest, rending all its stems,
Its branches severing.   The bison, reverend
Greybeard, did tremble in the moss, erected
The long hair of his mane, and half arose,
Leaned on his forelegs, shook his beard, and gazed
Bewildered on the embers, glimmering
On sudden 'mid the broken clods.   It was
A wandering grenade, that whirled around,

And raged, and hissed, and burst with thunder-
    noise.
The bison, for the first time in his life,
Felt fear, and to the deepest refuge fled.

"A battle! where? In what part?" asked the youths.
They seized their weapons, women raise their hands
To heaven; all sure of victory, with tears
Cry, " Heaven is with Napoleon, he with us!"

O spring! I, who beheld thee in our land,
Spring-time renowned for war! spring-time of
    beauty!
O spring! I, who beheld thee blossoming
With corn and grass, and gleaming all with men,
Fruitful in doings, pregnant thou with hope,
I see thee yet, fair phantom of a dream!—
In slavery born, chained yet in infancy,
I had but one such spring-time in my life!

.   .   .   .   .   .

Right by the high-road Soplicowo lay,
Whereby two leaders marched from Niemen's side,[1]
Prince Joseph and Jerome, Westphalia's King.
They had already conquered part of Litva,

From Grodno unto Slonim, when the King
Commanded three days' halt to breathe the troops.
But spite of weariness the Polish soldiers
Lamented that the King forbade their march,
So gladly they would reach the Muscovite.

The Prince's chief staff in the neighbouring town
Was quartered, but in Soplicowo stood
The camp of forty thousand, with their staffs;
The Generals Dombrowski, Kniaziewicz,
And Malachowski, Giedroic, Grabowski.

Late was it when they entered; therefore each
Where best he might found quarters--in the castle,
And in the mansion.   Orders swift were given;
The sentinels were posted; each man, wearied,
Went to his chamber for repose;—with night
All things were silent, camp, and house, and field.
Alone were seen, like shadows, wandering
Patrols, and here and there the camp-fires' gleam,
And circling watch-words heard of army posts.

All slept—the master of the house, the leaders,
And soldiers.   But the Wojski's eyes alone
Taste no sweet sleep; the Wojski must set forth

Next day a banquet, whereby he will make
Soplica's house renowned for evermore ;
A banquet dear to hearts of Polish guests,
And suiting a great day's solemnity,
Feast of the Church, and of the family.
To-morrow shall three couples be betrothed ;
But General Dombrowski yester-eve
Had said he wished to have a Polish dinner.

Though late the hour, the Wojski gathered quick
Cooks from the neighbourhood ; of these were
    five.
They serve, he plays the master.   As chief cook,
He girded him with apron white, indued
A white cap, and his sleeves to elbow rolled.
In one hand was his fly-scare, to drive off
The miserable insects, greedily
Upon the tit-bits falling ; with the other
He wiped his spectacles and put them on,
Drew forth a book, and opened it, and read.

The book entitled was, "The Perfect Cook." [2]
Therein all specialties were plainly written
Of Polish tables ; after its direction
The Count of Tenczyn those famed banquets gave

In Italy, whereat the Holy Father,
Urban the Eighth, so marvelled.[3]   After them
Charles Radziwill, " Belovèd," later on,
When he in Nieswiez King Stanislas
Received, that memorable banquet made,
Whose glory even now through Litva lives
In story of the people.
                              What the Wojski
Reading did understand, and did explain,
The cooks intelligent at once fulfilled.
The labour seethes, some fifty knives are clattering
Upon the board, the scullions bustle round,
As demons black ; some carry wood, some jugs
With wine and milk, they pour it into kettles,
Stewpans, and saucepans.   Smoke bursts forth; two
     scullions
Beside the oven sit, and blow the bellows.
The Wojski, that the wood might easier burn,
Commanded melted butter to be poured
Upon the wood—permitted such excess
Is in a wealthy house.   The scullions heap
Upon the fire dry brushwood ; others place
Upon the spits enormous roasts of beef,
Of venison, quarters of the boar and stag ;
Some pluck great heaps of birds, the feathers fly

In clouds—grouse, heathcocks, chickens, all are
    stripped.
But fowls were not in plenty ; since that inroad
Which at the period of the foray made
The murderous young Dobrzynski on the henhouse
When he Sophia's care reduced to nought,
Nor left of reparation means, not yet
In Soplicowo, once renowned for poultry,
The birds again might flourish.   For the rest
Of every kind of meat was great abundance,
Which might be gathered there from house and
    shambles,
And from the forests and the neighbourhood,
From near and far ;—thou'dst say the only thing
They could not furnish forth was milk of birds.*
Two things a liberal master seeks in feasts
Were joined in Soplicowo, art and plenty.

Already had arisen the solemn day ;
The weather was most fair, the hour was early,
And the clear heaven was drawn around the earth
Like to a hanging sea, still, concave-arched.
A few stars glimmered from the deep, like pearls

---

* A proverb, used to imply great abundance and luxury.

From sea-depths through the billows; on one side
A white cloud, one alone, flies lightly upward,
And in the deep-blue sky were plunged its wings,
Like parting pinions of a guardian angel,
Who by the nightly prayer of men detained,
And over-late, hastes to return among
His fellow-denizens of heaven.

                        Now quenched
The last faint pearls of stars, and in the depths
Of skies extinguished were, and heaven's brow
Is paler midmost.   Its right temple, laid
Upon a pillow of shade, is swarthy still;
The left aye redder blushes; farther off,
A circle, like an eyelid broad, opes wide,
And in the midst the white part of an eye
Is seen, the iris and the pupil; now
A sunbeam darted forth, and in the round
Of skies it gleamed refracted, and it hung
Upon a white cloud like a golden lance.
Upon this arrow, signal of the day,
A sheaf of fires flew forth, a thousand rockets,
That o'er the circle of the world did cross.
And rose the sun's eye.   Somewhat yet asleep,
It winked, and trembling shook its radiant lashes,
Shining at once with all its seven hues.

At once it shone with sapphire, redly glowed
In ruby, yellow with the topaz light ;
Till all at once it flamed as crystal clear.
Then like a gleaming diamond : lastly fiery,
Like to a great moon, like a twinkling star ;
Thus through the heavens measureless did pass
The lonely sun.
          To-day the Litvin people
From all the neighbourhood are gathered round
The chapel ere the sunrise, as to hear
The announcement of some novel miracle.
This gathering from the people's piety
In part proceeded, part from curiousness ;
For this day will the generals be present
At mass in Soplicowo, those renowned
As leaders of our legions, they of whom
The people knew the names, and honoured them
Like patron saints, and all whose wanderings,
Campaigns, and battles were a national
Gospel to Litva.
          Now some officers
Had come already, and a crowd of soldiers.
The people flocked around them, on them gazed,
And scarcely might believe their eyes, beholding
Their fellow-countrymen in uniform,

Armed, free, and speaking in the Polish tongue.
Mass was performed.   The tiny sanctuary
Might not contain the whole assembly there ;
The people kneel upon the grass, and gaze
Inside the chapel doors, uncovering
Their heads.   The hair of the Litvanian folk,
Fair-hued or yellow, golden shone like field
Of ripened rye ; and blooming here and there
The fair hair of a maiden, with fresh flowers
Adorned, or peacock's eyes, with ribbons braided,
Adornment of the tresses, gleamed among
The men's heads, as 'mid wheat corn-flowers and
    tares.
The many-coloured, kneeling crowd o'erspread
The field, and at the bell's voice. as it were
At blowing of the wind, the heads all bowed,
As corn-ears in a field.
             The village maids
To-day unto our Lady's altar bear
Spring's earliest gifts, fresh branches of green herbs ;
All round in garlands and in nosegays dressed,
Altar and picture, and the belfry even,
And galleries.   At times the morning breeze,
When blowing from the east, the garlands strips,
And throws on brows of kneeling worshippers,

And scatters them like fragrance from the censers.
But when the Mass and sermon both were done,
Presiding o'er the whole assembly now
The Chamberlain came forth, elected Marshal,[4]
With one accord, by all the District's States,
Wearing the Palatinal uniform,
A *zupan* gold-embroidered, the *kontusz*
Of Tours brocade with fringes, massy girdle,
Where hung a sabre with a shagreen hilt,
And a great diamond pin gleamed at his neck.
White his Confederate cap, and thereupon
A bunch of precious feathers ; crests were these
Of herons white ; on festivals alone
Is worn so rich a plume, whose every feather
A ducat costs.   Thus clad, upon a hill
Before the church he mounted.   Round him
      pressed
The villagers and soldiers.   Thus he spoke :

" Brothers, the priest has late to you proclaimed
The freedom which the Emperor-king restored
Unto the crown, and now to Litva's Duchy ;
Restored unto all Poland ; ye have heard
The government decrees, and convocation
Summoning the Diet.   I have but to speak

A few words to the people, on a matter
Concerning the Soplica family,
Lords of this place.

        " The region all remembers
The crime committed by the late Pan Jacek
Soplica here ; but since you all do know
His crimes, 'tis time we likewise should proclaim
His merits to the world.   The leaders of
Our armies here are present, from whom I
Have learned all that which now I tell to you.
This Jacek did not die, as rumour said,
In Rome, but only changed his former life,
And state, and name, and all his crimes against
God and the Fatherland he has effaced
By holy life, and by great deeds.

           " 'Twas he,
At Hohenlinden, who, when General Richepanse,
Half-beaten, did bethink him of retreat,
Unknowing Kniaziewicz with help drew near ;—
He, Jacek, Robak called, through swords and spears,
Bore letters from Kniaziewicz to Richepanse,
Announcing our men took the foe in rear.[5]
He later on in Spain, when that our lancers
Did capture Somosierra's trenchèd crest,[6]
At Kozieltulski's side was wounded twice.

Then, as an envoy, charged with secret orders,
To different regions travelled he, to sound
The spirit of the people, to unite
Secret societies, and form them.   Lastly,
In Soplicowo, his paternal nest,
When he an insurrection did prepare,
He perished in a foray.   Just upon
His death intelligence to Warsaw came,
His Majesty the Emperor had deigned
To give him for his late heroic deeds
The ensigns chivalrous of Honour's Legion.*

" Wherefore all these things having in regard,
I, representing here the Wojewode's rule,
With my Confederation staff, proclaim
To you, that Jacek by his faithful service,
And by the Emperor's favour, has effaced
The stain of infamy, and now returns
To honour, and again he finds a place
In ranks of truest patriots.   Therefore who
Shall dare remind the family of Jacek
Of his long-expiated fault, shall fall
Beneath the punishment of such reproach,

---

* *Legion d'honneur.*

As *gravis notæ maculæ* declare,
The statute's words ; such penalty affects
Both *militem* and *scartabel*,[7] who shall
Put infamy upon a citizen ;
And since equality does now prevail,
Burghers and peasants this third article
Likewise obliges.*   Let this Marshal's order
The district Writer in the general Acts
Inscribe, and let the Wozny set it forth.

" As touches now the cross of Honour's Legion,
That it arrived too late shall not detract
From glory.   If it might not Jacek serve
As ornament, be it a memory of him.
Let us suspend it on his grave.   Three days
Let it hang here ; then in the chapel lay
The cross, a votive offering to the Virgin."

This saying, the order from its covering
He drew, and hung upon the humble cross
That marked the grave a crimson ribbon, tied
In form of a cockade, and that white cross,
Glittering with stars and with its golden crown.

---

* The inhabitants of cities only received full political privi-
leges by the constitution of 1791.

And in the sunbeams brightly shone the stars,
Like the last gleam of Jacek's earthly glory.
Meanwhile the people said upon their knees
The Angelus, for peace eternal praying
Unto the sinner's soul.   The Judge addressed
The guests and village crowd, inviting all
To Soplicowo for the banquet.

But

Upon the grassy bank before the house
Two old men sat, two measures full of mead
Upon their knees ; they towards the orchard gaze,
Where like a sunflower, 'mid the poppy-buds
Of various hue, there stood a lancer, wearing
A shining *kolpak*, decked with golden metal
And a cock's feather ; near to him a girl
In dress as green as lowly rue, upraised
Eyes blue as heart's-ease flowers towards the lad's.
Young maidens in the garden further off,
Were gathering flowers ; purposely they turned
Their heads away from where the lovers stood,
So that they might not trouble their discourse.

But those two old men drank their mead, and from
A snuff-box made of bark regaled each other,
And talked.

              "Yes, yes, dear old Protasy," said
Gervasy, Klucznik.—"Yes, dear old Gervasy,"
Protasy, Wozny, said.—"Yes, yes, just so,"
They in accord repeated many times,
Nodding their heads thereto.   At length the Wozny:
"That wondrously this suit has ended I
Do not deny, yet there are precedents ;
I can remember lawsuits during which
Far worse excesses happened than in ours,
But intermarriage ended all the evil.
Lopot to the Borzdobohaci
Was reconciled, the Krepsztuls to the house
Of Kupsc, and to Pikturna Putrament ;
Mackiewicz to the Odyniec family,
And Turno unto the Kwileckis.   But
What say I ?   Why, the Poles were used to have
With Litva disagreements worse by far
Than those of the Horeszkos and Soplica ;
But Queen Jadwiga, when she counsel took,
Did quickly end that feud without the courts.
'Tis well when parties have a maid or widow
To give in marriage, thus a compromise
Is always ready.   Lawsuits always last
The longest with the clergy, or with kindred
Too near related, for the action then

May never be with marriage brought to end.
Thence come the unending feuds of Poles and
 Russians,
Since they proceed from Lech and Russ, own
 brothers ; [8]
Thence were so many Lithuanian suits
With the Crusaders, till Jagellon won.
Thence, to conclude, *pendebat* long before
The acts, that famous lawsuit of the Rymszas
With the Dominicans, whence rose the proverb,
'The Lord is greater than Pan Rymsza.' But
I'll warrant, mead is better than the Penknife."
This saying, he clinked his goblet with the
 Klucznik's.

"True, true," replied Gervasy, greatly moved ;
"Wondrous have been the fortunes of our Crown,
And of our Litva ! Truly, like two consorts,
Heaven did unite them, and the devil part.
To Heaven his own, and to the devil his.
Ah ! brother dear, Protasy, that our eyes
Should see this ! that these dwellers of the Crown
Salute us ! I served with them years ago,
I well remember they were brave Confederates.
If but the Pantler, my late master, had

Lived to behold this day ! O Jacek ! Jacek !
But why should we lament ? This very day
Our Litva once more joineth with the Crown.
That too is reconciled, is blotted out."

" And this a wonder is," Protasy said,
" Concerning this Sophia, for whose hand
Our Thaddeus now entreats—a year ago
There was an omen, like a sign from Heaven."
" Lady Sophia !" broke the Klucznik in,
" We now must call her, since she is grown up ;
She is not a little girl ; besides, she is
Of dignitary blood, the Pantler's grandchild.
However," did Protasy end, " there was
A sign prophetic of her destiny.
I saw the sign with mine own eyes. A year
Ago, our household on a holiday
Did sit here, drinking mead ; but as we looked,
Down from the gable fell two sparrows fighting.
Both were old cock-birds ; one, the younger, had
A patch of grey beneath the throat, the other
A black one ; they went scuffling through the
      court,
Still turning somersaults, until they rolled
Deep in the dust. We looked on, and meanwhile

The servants whispered to each other, ' Let
The black one be Horeszko, and the other
Soplica ;' so as often as the grey
Was uppermost, they cried, ' Long live Soplica !'
' Fie ! fie !   Horeszko coward !' and when he fell,
They cried, ' Up, up, Soplica ! give not in
Unto the magnate ; shame 'twere for a noble !'
Thus jesting did we wait to see who conquered.
But just then little Sophy, moved with pity
For those two birds, ran up, and covered o'er
Both heroes with her little hand ; they fought
Together in her hand, until their plumage
Flew wide, such rage was in those little devils !
The old women whispered, looking on Sophia,
That it was surely the girl's destiny
To reconcile two houses long at feud.
And now I see, to-day has rendered true
The old women's omen, though in truth they then
Were thinking of the Count, and not of Thaddeus."

Thereto the Klucznik answered : " Wonderful
Events are in this world ; who all can fathom ?
I'll also tell you something ; although not
So wondrous as that omen, yet 'tis hard
Of understanding.   Thou dost know, that once

I had been glad to drown the family
Of the Soplicas in a spoon of water; *
But yet this little fellow Thaddeus
I was extremely fond of from a child.
I saw that when he fought with other boys,
He always beat them ; so as oft as he
Ran to the castle, I would put him up
To some hard undertaking ; he did all.
Were it to get down pigeons from the tower,
Or pluck the mistletoe from off the oak,
Or plunder crows' nests from the highest pines,
He did it all !   I said unto myself—
' This lad is born beneath a lucky star ;
A pity 'tis that he is a Soplica !'
But who had guessed the castle should in him
Welcome its heir, the husband of my lady
Sophia, my most gracious mistress ? "
                                    Here
The old men left off their discourse, and drank,
Deep thinking ; only now and then were heard
These few short words—"Yes, yes, master Gervasy;"
" Yes, yes, master Protasy."
                              The green bank

---

* A proverb, signifying to be ready to avenge oneself on
the first occasion.—E. S. N.

Touched close upon the kitchen, whereof stood
The window open, and the steam burst forth,
As from a conflagration ; till from out
The wreaths of steam, like to a white dove, gleamed
The chief cook's white cap ; through the kitchen
    window
The Wojski o'er the old men's heads his own
Put forth, in silence listening their discourse ;
And offered them a saucer full of biscuits,
Saying, " Eat these with your mead, and I mean-
    while
Will tell to you a curious history
Of a dispute that well-nigh ended in
A bloody fight, when, hunting in the depths
Of Naliboko's forests, Rejtan played
A trick to Prince Denassau.   This same trick
He well-nigh paid for with his own life.   I
Composed the quarrel of these gentlemen,
As I will now relate to you." [9]   But here
The cooks broke off the Wojski's story, asking
Whom he had charged to arrange the centre-piece.

The Wojski went away, and having emptied
Their mead, the old men, in deep thought, their
    eyes

Turned to the garden depths, where held discourse
That handsome lancer with the maiden.   He
Just then within his left hand taking hers—
The right was in a sling, for he was wounded—
" Sophia, thou now must tell me once for all
Ere we change rings.   I must be sure of this.
What matter that last winter thou wert ready
To give thy word to me ?   I would not then
Accept that word.   For what to me availed
A promise forced ?   At that time I had stayed
Short time in Soplicowo.   I was not
So vain I could delude myself to thinking
That by one look of mine I could awake
Within thee love.   I am no coxcomb ; I
By mine own merits wished to gain thy love,
Though long I waited for it.   Now thou art
So gracious as to give once more thy word.
By what have I deserved so high a grace ?
Maybe thou takest me, Sophia, not
So much from inclination, only that
Thine uncle and thine aunt to this persuade thee.
But marriage is, Sophia, a weighty thing.
Advise with thine own heart ; in this attend
No threatenings of thine uncle, nor thine aunt's
Persuasions.   If thou feelest nought for me

But goodwill, we may this betrothal yet
Some time delay. I have no wish to bind
Thy will, and we will wait awhile, Sophia.
Nought hurries us, since yester evening I
Received commandment to remain in Litva,
Drill-master in the regiment here, until
My wounds be healed. What then, beloved
    Sophia ? "

Thereto Sophia answered, raising up
Her head, and looking shyly in his eyes :
" I do not well remember what occurred
Long since ; I know they all said that I must
Be married to you ; always I agree
With Heaven's will, and with my elders' wish."
Then dropping down her eyes, she added this :
" Before you parted, if you recollect,
When Friar Robak died that stormy night,
I saw that, in departing, you were grieved·
To leave us ; there were tears within your eyes.
Those tears, I tell you truly, sank within
My heart, so I believe you, that you love me.
As often as I prayed for your success,
You ever stood before me with those large
And shining tears. The Chamberlain's wife then

Went afterwards to Wilna, and she took me
There with her for the winter ; but I longed
For Soplicowo, and that little room,
Where first at eve you met me by the table ;
And then took leave.   I know not how, your
      memory,
Something like cabbage-seed in autumn sown,
Through all the winter quickened in my heart ;
That, as I said to you, unceasingly
I longed for that apartment, and to me
Did something whisper, I again should find
You there, and so it happened.   Having that
Within my heart, your name was often on
My lips ; 'twas during Carnival at Wilna ;
And the young ladies said I was in love.
Now if I some one loved, who should it be,
Excepting you ?"   Thaddeus, with such a proof
Of love delighted, took her by the hand,
Pressed it, and they together left the garden,
Went to that lady's bower, unto that room
Where Thaddeus had dwelt ten years ago.

Now there the Regent tarried, wondrously
Adorned, and served his fair betrothèd dame,
With running to and fro, and offering

Rings, chains, and pots, and flasks, cosmetics,
    perfumes ;
Joyful, he gazed with triumph on the bride.
The bride her toilette ended even now ;
She sat before a mirror, taking counsel
Of the divinities of grace ; the maids,
Some with the curling-irons renew the stiffened
Rings of the tresses, others, kneeling, labour
Upon the flounces.
            While the Regent thus
Near his betrothed was busy, at the window
A scullion knocked ; a hare had just been seen.
That hare, late stolen from the osiers forth,
Ran through the meadow, in the orchard sprang
Among the growing vegetables.   There
He sat, 'twere easy now to start him, and
To hunt him down, the greyhounds placing on
The clearing.   The Assessor hastens, dragging
By the collar Sokol ; after him makes haste
The Regent, calling Kusy.   Both the dogs
The Wojski stations by the hedge, but then
Betook him with his fly-scare to the orchard.
Trampling, and whistling, clapping, much he
    frightens
The game ; the prickers, each one by the collar

His greyhound holding, pointing where the hare
Is stirring, chuckled silently ; the dogs
Pricked up their ears impatiently, they trembled,
Like arrows twain upon one bowstring laid.
At once the Wojski gave the starting word ;
The hare straight darted from behind the hedge,
Upon the mead ; the greyhounds after him.
And presently, without a double, Sokol
And Kusy fell together on the hare,
From two sides in an instant, like a bird's
Two wings, and plunged into the creature's back
Their teeth-like claws ; the hare gave forth one cry,
Grievous, as of a new-born child.   The prickers
Rushed to the spot ; the hare now lifeless lies,
The greyhounds tear the white fur on his breast.

The prickers stroked their dogs ; meanwhile the
        Wojski
Drew from his girdle forth a hunting-knife,
Cut off the feet, and said, " To-day the dogs
Shall have an equal fee, for they have both
Won equal glory, equal both in swiftness,
Equal in labour ; ' Worthy is the palace
Of Pac, and Pac is worthy of the palace ; ' [10]
Worthy the prickers of their greyhounds, worthy

The greyhounds of their prickers.   Here, behold,
Your long and bitter quarrel now is done.
I, whom you chose as judge to hold your stakes,
Pronounce at length my sentence ; both of you
Have won ; the pledges I restore ; let each
Receive his own again, and both you sign
A peace."   Then at the old man's invitation
The prickers turned a joyous countenance
Upon each other, and together joined
Their right hands, long divided.

       Then the Regent
Said, " Once I staked a horse with all its
  trappings.
I notice gave before the local court,
That I deposited my ring as fee
Unto our Judge ; a pledge deposited,
Returned may not be.   Let the Wojski take
This ring as a remembrance, and command
His name to be thereon engraved, or, if
He will, Hreczecha's arms.   The bloodstone's
  smooth,
The gold was tried eleven times.   That steed
The lancers for the horse have requisitioned ;
But still the saddle has remained with me.
'Tis praised by every connoisseur, as being

Convenient, lasting, lovely as a toy.
The saddle, in the Turkish Cossack style,
Is narrow ; in the front a pommel is ;
Upon it precious stones, a cushion of
Rich stuff upon the seat ; and when you spring
Unto the saddle-bow, on this soft down
Between the pommels you may sit at ease
As on a couch ; and when you gallop "—here
Regent Bolesta, who, as well we know,
Loved gestures greatly, spread his legs apart,
As though he sprang on horseback, then presenting
A gallop, slowly rocked from side to side—
" And when you set off in a gallop, then
There beams a splendour from the saddle-bow,
As gold were dropping from the charger, for
The stirrup-bands are sprinkled o'er with gold,
And silver the broad stirrups gilded o'er.
Upon the mouth-piece reins, and on the bridle,
Shine little buttons of the pearly shell ;
And to the breast-piece hangs a moon in shape
Of Leliwa, that is, of the new moon,[11]
This splendid unique furniture—'twas captured,
Report says, in the battle of Podhajce,
From some considerable Turkish noble—
Receive, as proof of my regard, Assessor."

Whereto the Assessor answered, with the gift
Delighted : " I one time my beautiful
Dog-collars, given me by Prince Sanguszko,
Pledged ; made of shagreen, all with golden circles
Inlaid, and with a leash of silk, whereof
The workmanship is precious as the stone
That shines upon it.   I desired to leave
This set an heirloom to my children—certain
I shall have children, as I shall be married,
Thou knowest, to-day.   But, Regent, be so good
As to accept this set, I pray, in change
For thy rich furniture, and in remembrance
Of this dispute, which has prevailed for years,
And has at last so honourably come
To end for both of us.   Let peace now flourish
Between us."   So they home returned, to announce
At table that the contest between Sokol
And Kusy now was ended.
                                    Stories were
The Wojski in the house had nurtured up
This hare, and secretly had let it loose
Into the garden, so to make agreed
The prickers by such conquest, far too light.
The old man with such mystery performed
The trick that he completely had deceived

All Soplicowo.   Some years later something
The scullion of this whispered, to renew
The Assessor's quarrel with the Regent, but
In vain he spread such tales to wrong the dogs;
The Wojski still denied it, and none then
Believed the scullion.

                 Now the guests assembled
In the great banquet-hall, the banquet waiting,
Conversed around the table, when the Judge
Entered, in Palatinal uniform,
And led in Master Thaddeus and Sophia.
Thaddeus, his forehead with the left hand touching,
Saluted with a soldier's bow his leaders.
Sophia, with glances cast upon the earth,
Blushing, the guests with curtsy welcomed, taught
By Telimena now to curtsy well.
She wore a garland on her head, in sign
Of spousal; for the rest, her dress was such
As when to-day within the chapel she
Laid spring sheaves for the Virgin.   She once
      more
Had reaped fresh bunches for the guests of herbs;
With one hand she distributes flowers and grass,
The other hand adjusts the shining sickle
Upon her head.   The leaders took the herbs,

Kissing her hands.   Sophia once again
Curtsied all round, deep blushing.

General

Kniaziewicz then raised her in his arms,
And printing on her brow a father's kiss,
Raised up the girl, and set her on the table.
Applauding, all cried, " Bravo ! " all enchanted
With the girl's beauty, but especially
By her Litvanian dress, its simpleness ;
Since for these leaders, who in wandering life,
So long in foreign parts throughout the world,
Had journeyed, wondrous charms the native dress
Possessed, as it recalled to them their youth,
And former loves.   Therefore, well-nigh with tears,
They thronged around the table ; eagerly
They gazed.   Some pray Sophia would uplift
Her head a little, and would show her eyes ;
Some that she condescend to turn around.
The bashful maiden turned, but with her hands
Still veiled her eyes.   Most joyful, Thaddeus gazed,
And rubbed his hands together.

Whether some one

Had given Sophia counsel to appear
In such a dress, or she by instinct knew—
For every girl by instinct can divine

What suits her countenance—it is enough
That for the first time in her life Sophia
This morning was by Telimena scolded
For her self-will, no fashionable dress
Desiring, until she by tears prevailed
That she might thus be left, in simple dress.

She had a long, white petticoat, the dress
Short, of green camlet, with a rosy hem;
The bodice likewise green, with rosy ribbons,
Laced cross-wise from the bosom to the neck,
The bosom underneath, hid like a bud
Beneath a leaf; white from the shoulders gleamed
The shift-sleeves, like the wings of butterflies
Expanded for their flight; these at the wrist
Were gathered, and with ribbon fastened there.
The neck was likewise by the narrow shift
Surrounded, with its collar girded up
By a rosy breast-knot; earrings artfully
Carved out of cherry-stones, whose fashioning
Had been Dobrzynski's pride; two tiny hearts
Were there, with dart and flame, given to Sophia,
When Bustard wooed her.   And upon the collar
There hung two strings of amber.   On her shoulders
Sophia had thrown the ribbons of her tresses,

And on her forehead placed, as reapers wont,
A curvèd sickle, polished recently
By reaping grass, bright, like the crescent moon
Upon Diana's brow.

                        All praised, all clapped.
One of the officers from out his pocket
Drew a portfolio, with some folds of paper.
He spread them out, his pencil sharpened, moist-
    ened,
Looked on Sophia, and drew. Scarce saw the
    Judge
The paper and the pencil, when he knew
The sketcher, though a Colonel's uniform,
Rich epaulettes, a truly lancer mien,
A darkened moustache, and a Spanish beard
Had changed him greatly, yet the Judge him knew.
" How are you, my Illustrious, gracious Count ?
And have you in your cartridge-box your travelling
Painting materials ? " 'Twas the Count indeed ;
Not long a soldier, but because he owned
Large revenues, and at his own expense
A regiment had of cavalry equipped,
And in the first fight borne him gallantly,
The Emperor on that day had named him Colonel.
So did the Judge salute the Count, and on

His rank congratulated him ; the Count
Heard nothing, but still drew with diligence.

Meanwhile the second pair betrothed came in.
The Assessor, once the Czar's, to-day Napoleon's
Devoted servant ; under his command
He had a body of gendarmes, and though
Scarce twenty hours in office, he already
Wore the grey uniform with Polish facings,
And dragged a crooked sabre at his side,
And clinked his spurs.   With stately step beside
    him,
Came his beloved, magnificently dressed,
Thekla Hreszczanka, for the Assessor long
Had cast off Telimena, and as more
To sadden this coquette, his true affections
Had turned towards the Wojszczanka now.
Not over-young the bride was, she well-nigh
Reached middle age, but a good manager,
With dignity and dowry ; for besides
A hamlet she inherited, the Judge
Her dowry by a small sum had increased.

The third pair vainly they long time await :
The Judge impatient grew, and servants sent.

Returning, these bring answer, the third bridegroom,
The Regent, starting forth the hare, had lost
The ring; he sought it in the meadow, and
The Regent's lady, though herself she hastes,
And though the serving-women her assist,
Cannot by any means her toilette end.
She scarcely will at four o'clock be ready.

NOTES TO BOOK XI.

1. "*Whereby two leaders marched from Niemen's side.*"

The French and Polish armies crossed the Niemen on the 24th June 1812.

2. "*The book entitled was, 'The Perfect Cook.'*"

* A book now extremely rare, published by Stanislaw Czernicki.

3. "*Those famous banquets,*" &c.

* This Roman embassy has been often described. See "The Perfect Cook," preface. "This legation, being a great marvel to all the Western empire, proclaimed a lord unsurpassed in wit, by the splendour of the house and the service of the table, so that one of the Roman princes said, 'To-day Rome is happy in possessing such an ambassador.'"

4. "*Elected Marshal,*" &c.

* In Lithuania, on the entrance of the French and Polish armies, Confederations were formed in the palatinates, and deputies elected to the Diet.

5. "*Announcing our men took the foe in rear.*"

* It is well known that a Polish corps, under the leadership of General Kniaziewicz, at Hohenlinden, decided the victory.

6. " *When that our lancers*
Did capture Somosierra's trenchèd crest."

The capture of Somosierra, by which the road to Madrid
was left open to Napoleon's troops, was accomplished on
the 30th November 1808. After several unsuccessful assaults,
owing to the obstinate resistance of the Spaniards, a body
of Polish lancers and sharpshooters was despatched against
the chief entrenchments. After covering the ground with
their dead, they captured the Spanish artillery, and thereby
supported, dislodged the defenders. The Spanish commander,
San Juan, with great difficulty cut his way through the
Poles, and reached Segovia at imminent hazard.—Toreño,
Guerra i Revolucion en España.

7. " *Both* militem *and* scartabel."

The meaning of *militem* is obvious. *Scartabel* is one of
those terms not easy to define. It has many classical deriva-
tions assigned to it, with which it is hardly worth while to
trouble the reader. Linde thinks that it is a term used to
express a new nobility, who owe their rank to fortune in
war, from the right to be ennobled which a soldier by a
law of Stephen Batory might claim after a certain amount
of service, and which was often granted. Or *scartabelli* might
be nobles living under citizen law. Czacki says : " The *scarta-
bellus* hold a midway position between the ancient nobility
and those who have risen from being peasants."—*Linde.*

8. " *Since they proceed from Lech and Russ, own brothers.*"

The three brothers Czech, Lech, and Russ were the
legendary founders of the Bohemian, Polish, and Russian
peoples. (See *Le Monde Slave*, by Cyprien Robert.)

9. *" As I will now relate to you."*

* Prince Denassau's real name was the Duke of Nassau-Siegen, a noted warrior and adventurer. He was Russian admiral, and defeated the Turks, and was himself defeated by the Swedes. He remained for some time in Poland, where he obtained letters of nobility. His single combat with a tiger (in Africa ! !) was much celebrated in all the gazettes of Europe.

The story which the Wojski never finished, concerning Rejtan's quarrel with the Prince of Nassau, is known from tradition. Rejtan, offended by the prince's boasting, once stood beside him on a clearing. Just then a monstrous wild boar, furious with shot wounds, and with being hunted, rushed upon them. Rejtan snatched the prince's gun from his hands, threw it on the ground, and taking a spear, and giving another to the German, said, "Now let us see which of us can manage a spear best." The boar was just rushing upon them, when the Wojski Hreczecha, standing at a distance, slew the beast by a fortunate shot. The gentlemen were at first angry, but afterwards became reconciled to each other, and liberally rewarded Hreczecha.

10. *" Worthy is the palace*
Of Pac, and Pac is worthy of the palace."

One of the finest palaces in Warsaw is that of General Pac, who died at Smyrna in exile. The Russians converted it into a bazaar of industry.

11. *" A moon in shape*
Of Leliwa, that is, of the new moon."

The Leliwa is a crest of Polish heraldry, and is the horizontal crescent with a star between its horns.

BOOK XII.

—————

LET US LOVE ONE ANOTHER.

The last old-Polish banquet—The Arch-service—Explanation
of its figures—Its movements—Dombrowski receives a pre-
sent—More about the Penknife—Kniaziewicz receives a pre-
sent—First exercise of authority by Thaddeus on taking
possession—Observations by Gervasy—A concert of concerts
—The Polonaise—Let us love one another.

AT length the doors flew open with loud noise.
The Wojski entered in a cap, with head
Upraised, he nor saluted, nor took place
At table, for the Wojski cometh forth
In a new semblance ; marshal of the court,
He bears a wand in sign of office ; with
That wand he points to all a seat, and places
The guests in turn.   First, as the highest ruler
Within the district, took the Chamberlain-
Marshal the seat of honour, velvet chair,
With ivory arms !   Beside him, on the right,

Sat General Dombrowski, on the left
Were Kniaziewicz, and Pac, and Malachowski;
'Mid them the lady of the Chamberlain.
Then other ladies, officers and lords,
Nobles and country people, men and women,
Alternately, by couples, sit in order,
Where'er the Wojski indicates.

       The Judge,
Saluting, left the banquet. In the courtyard
He must regale the peasant company.
Behind a table he had gathered them
Two furlongs long; himself sat at one end,
And at the other sat the parish priest.
Thaddeus and Sophia did not sit
At table; busied with the entertaining,
They ate while walking; 'twas an ancient custom,
At the first banquet, that the new possessors
Themselves should serve the people.

       In the meantime
The guests, while dishes waited in the hall,
On the great centre-piece astonished looked,
Its metal precious as the workmanship.
Tradition says Prince Radziwill the Orphan
Had caused this set in Venice to be made,
And from his own designs to be adorned,

In Polish fashion.   Then the centre-piece
Was captured in the Swedish war; it came,
None knew in what way, to a noble house.
To-day, it had been taken from the treasury,
And occupied the middle of the board
With its great circle, as a cart-wheel broad.   '

The service was o'erlaid, from depth to border,
With froth and sugar snowy-white ; it showed
A winter landscape excellently well.
In midst rose black a mighty sweetmeat grove ;
Around were houses like to villages,
And nobles' farmsteads,* spread with sugar froth
Instead of rime-frost; on the margin stood
Vessels for ornament, small personages,
Fashioned of porcelain, in Polish dresses,
And like to actors on a stage they seemed
Presenting some events ; their gesture given
Most artfully, the colours vivid, voice
Alone they wanted, otherwise alive.

"What should these represent?" the guests inquired.
Thereon the Wojski raised his wand on high,

---

* The original words are *wioski* and *zascianki*, both of
which have been already explained.

And thus discoursed—meanwhile was *wódka* given,
Before they ate—" By the permission of
The gracious gentlemen, these personages
That here you countless see, present a history
Of Polish *sejmiks*, councils, voting, triumphs,
And quarrels.   I myself this scene imagined,
And will explain it to you.

           " Here, to right,
You see a numerous crowd of noblemen
Before the Diet to a banquet asked.
The table waiteth covered ; no one seats
The guests ; they stand in groups, each group
    takes counsel.
Look, in the midst of every group there stands
A man, whose opened lips, whose lifted eyes,
Unquiet hands, denote the orator.
Explaining somewhat, with his finger he
Doth emphasise his speaking, with his hand
He illustrates his meaning.   Here are speakers
Who recommend their candidate, with various
Success, as from their brother nobles' mien
You may perceive.

           " True, in this second group
The nobles list attentive, this one plants
His hands upon his girdle, lends his ear.

That one his hand holds to his ear, and twirls
In silence his moustache ; he probably
Collects the words, and in his memory strings
    them.
The orator rejoices, for he sees
They are convinced, and stroketh down his pouch.
He has their votes already in his pouch.

" But in the third assembly other things
Are passing.   Here the orator must seize
The hearers by their girdles.   Look, they wrest
Themselves away, retire their ears.   Look how
This hearer swells with rage ; he lifts his hands,
Threatens the orator, and stops his mouth,
Hearing, no doubt, the praises of his rival ;
This other, stooping like a bull his head,
You'd say to take the speaker on his horns ;
Some draw their sabres, some take to their heels.

" One noble silent stands among the groups ;
We see he is an independent man.
He hesitates and fears,—how shall he vote ?
Not knowing, and in conflict with himself,
He asks of fate, he lifts his hand, puts forth
The forefingers, half-shuts his eyes, with nail

Takes aim at nail; this conjuring will confirm
His vote, for if the fingers meet, he gives
A vote affirmative, but if they miss,
He casts a negative.

                    " The left presents
Another scene—a convent dining-hall,
Turned to a hall of meeting of the nobles.
The elders on a bench sit in a row,
The young men stand, and gaze with eagerness
Betwixt the heads towards the centre. Midmost
The Marshal stands; in hand he holds the urn,
He counts the balls, the nobles with their eyes
Devour them, in this instant he has shaken
The last one out; the heralds lift their hands,
Proclaim the elected legislator's name.

" One nobleman heeds not the general concord.
Look, from the window of the convent kitchen
He thrusts his head; look how his eyes start
      forth;
How bold he looks, how wide he opes his lips,
As though he would the chamber all devour.
Easy it is to guess this nobleman
Has cried out, "Veto!" Look how, at this sudden
Kindling of quarrel, to the doors the throng

Rush, to the kitchen certainly they go ;
They have drawn their sabres, sure a bloody
    fight
Will now begin.
                    " But in the corridor,
Consider, gentlemen, this ancient priest,
Who wears a cope.   This is the prior ; he bears
The Host from off the altar ; and a boy,
Clad in a surplice, sounds a bell, and craves
Admission ; presently the nobles sheathe
Their sabres, cross themselves, and kneel.   The
    priest
Turns to that quarter where the sword yet clashes.
Soon as he comes all peaceful is and still.

" Ah ! you, young sirs, cannot remember this,
How 'mid our stormy and free-ruling nobles,
All armed, no need at all was of police ;
While faith was flourishing and laws respected,
Then freedom was with order, and abundance
Of glory !   But in other lands, I hear,
The government maintaineth soldiery,
Police, gendarmes, and constables ; but if
The sword alone can guard the public safety,
That in these lands is Freedom I believe not."

Just then, upon his snuff-box tapping, spoke
The Chamberlain : " Sir Wojski, please to lay
Aside till later on these histories.
Truly the *sejmik* is most interesting,
But we are hungry.   Order that the dishes
Be brought in."
        Thereunto the Wojski, lowering
His wand unto the ground : " Illustrious,
Most Powerful Chamberlain, allow me pray
This favour.   I will end at once the last
Scene of these diets.   Here is the new Marshal,
Borne by his partisans from the refect'ry.
Look how the brother nobles throw their caps
Aloft, they ope their lips to cry, ' Long live !'
But there, upon the other side, the noble
Outvoted, lonely, on his moody brow
Has pressed his cap.   His wife before the house
Awaits him ; she has guessed what late occurred.
Poor woman ! in her servant's arms she faints !
Poor woman ! for she thought to have the title,
Illustrious, Most Powerful ; but again
For three years she is only a Most Powerful."

The Wojski ended his description here,
And gave a signal with his wand.   And soon

With dishes lackeys entered, two and two ;
The soups, the *barszcz,** called royal, and the
    rosol †
Of ancient Poland, artfully prepared ;
Thereto the Wojski had with wondrous secrets
Cast in some small pearls, and a piece of money.
Such *rosol* purifies the blood, and health
Doth fortify. Then followed other dishes ;—
But who shall tell their names ? who understand
These, in our times already quite unknown ?—
Those fishes, salmon from the Danube, dried,
Venetian and Turkish caviare,
Soles, carp, and mackerel, pike and "noble
    carp."
At last a mystery of cookery,
A fish uncut, fried slightly at the head,
And roasted in the centre, at the tail
Some preparation made with sauce.
                   The guests
Nor asked the names of all these dishes, nor
That wondrous secret stayed them ; quick they
    ate

---

* A soup made chiefly of beet-root and cream.
† *Consommé.*

All things with soldiers' appetite, and filled
Their goblets up with wine of Hungary.

But in the meantime the great service [1] changed
Its colour ; bare of snow, it now looked green.
For that light sugary froth, now gradually
Warmed   by   the   summer's   heat,   had   melted,
      and
The under side discovered, hitherto
Concealèd from the eye ; and so the landscape
Presented a new season of the year.
It shone with green and many-coloured spring ;
There came forth various grains, as on the ways
They grow ; the saffron wheat luxuriant,
With golden ears, the rye with silver leaves,
And buckwheat, formed by art, of chocolate,
And pear and apple orchards blossoming.

The guests have scarcely time to enjoy the gifts
Of summer ; vainly they entreat the Wojski
But to prolong them, for the service now
Like to the planet, in its destined orbit,
Changes its season ; now the painted grains,
Golden, have gathered warmth within the room,
And gradually melt, the grass turns yellow,

The leaves turn red, and fall; thou wouldst have
    said
An autumn wind was blowing; at the last
Those trees, late well-adorned, appearing stripped
By storm-winds and by hoar frost, naked stand.
They were but twigs of cinnamon, or branches
Of bay twigs, counterfeiting pine-trees, dressed
With needles, that were seeds of carraway.

The guests, while drinking, stript the branches off
The stems and bark, and ate them with their wine.
The Wojski viewed his service all around,
And full of joy triumphant glances turned
Upon the guests.
            Henry Dombrowski showed
Immense astonishment, and said, " Sir Wojski,
Were those Chinean shadows? has Pineti
Given you his devils to your service? [2] are
Such services in general use in Litva?
Do all hold banquets with such ancient customs?
Pray tell me; I have spent my life abroad."

The Wojski answered, bowing : " No, Illustrious,
Most Powerful General, no godless art
Is this. 'Tis but a memory of those feasts,

Renowned in lordly houses of old times,
When Poland happiness and power enjoyed.
What I have done I gathered from this book.
Thou askest, whether everywhere in Litva
This custom is preserved. Alas ! new fashions
Among us even have crept in.   Not one
Young lord cries out, he suffers no excess ;
So like a Jew he stints his guests in meat,
And drink ; will grudge Hungarian wine, and drink
Satanic, falsified, and modern wines
Of Muscovy, Champagne ; then in the evening
Loses at cards full gold enough to give
A banquet to a hundred brother nobles.
Why, even—for what is in my heart to-day
I'll truly speak, let but the Chamberlain
Not take this ill of me—when I drew out
This wondrous service from the treasury,
Why, even the Chamberlain did laugh at me,
And said it was a wearisome machine,
An old-world thing, it seemed a toy for children,
Unsuitable to such illustrious men.
The Judge ! the Judge said, it would tire the guests.
And ne'ertheless, from that astonishment
I caused you, gentlemen, I well perceive
That this fine art was worthy to be seen.

I know not if another such occasion
Will come to entertain in Soplicowo
Such dignitaries.   I see, General,
You knowledge have of banquets.   Pray accept
This book.   It will be useful to you when
You give a banquet to a company
Of foreign monarchs, bah ! ev'n to Napoleon !
But let me, ere I consecrate this book
To you, relate the chance whereby it fell
Into my hands."

              This instant rose a murmur
Outside the door, together many voices
Cried, " Long live Weathercock ! "   Into the hall
A crowd did press, with Matthew at their head.
The Judge his guest conducted to the board,
And placed him high among the generals,
And said, " Sir Matthew, you are no good neigh-
    bour,
You have arrived too late, when dinner is
Nigh over."—" I am early," said Dobrzynski.
" I came not here for eating, but because
I had the curiosity to view
Our national army nearer.   There is much
To talk of, but 'tis neither here nor there.
The nobles saw and dragged me here by force,

And you have seated me at table.　Thanks, ·
My neighbour."　Having said this, upside down
He turned his plate, as sign he would not eat,
And kept a gloomy silence.

　　　　　　　　" Friend Dobrzynski,"
Said to him General Dombrowski, " you
Are that renownèd swordsman of Kosciuszko,
That Matthew called the Rod.　I know you from
Your fame.　But, prithee, how art thou preserved
So vigorous, so active ? what long years
Have passed away.　Look, I am growing old,
Look, even Kniaziewicz is somewhat grey,
But thou might'st hold thine own with young
　　men still.
And does thy Rod yet flourish as ere time ?
I heard that thou didst discipline the Russians
Not long ago.　But where are now thy brothers ?
I should exceedingly rejoice to see
Those Penknives, and your Razors, last examples
Of ancient Lithuania."

　　　　　　　　" General,"
Replied the Judge, " after that victory,
Nearly the whole of the Dobrzynskis took
Refuge within the Duchy, probably
They went into some legion."—" Ay, indeed,"

Said a young officer of squadron, " I
Have in the second company a whiskered
Scarecrow, Dobrzynski, who doth call himself
The Sprinkler, but the Polish soldiers call him
The Lithuanian Bear.   But if the General
Commands it, we will fetch him here."—"There
     are,"
Said a lieutenant, " others by their race
Of Litva, one a soldier, called by name
The Razor, and one more who with a trombone
Rides on the flank ; and also in a regiment
Of shooters, two Dobrzynskis, grenadiers."

" But, but—about their chief," the General
Replied ; " I wish to know about this Penknife,
Of which the Wojski told me such great wonders,
As of some giant of the elder time."
" The Penknife," said the Wojski, " though he went
Not into exile, yet as fearing inquest,
Concealed himself from search of Muscovites.
The poor man wandered all the winter long
Among the forests, lately he came forth.
He might be useful in these warlike times,
For 'tis a valiant man, 'tis only pity
He's somewhat pressed by age.   But there he is."

The Wojski pointed in the hall, where stood
Servants and village folk together crowded.
But over all the heads gleamed suddenly
A shining bald pate, like to a full moon.
Three times it issued forth, and three times van-
　　ished
Amid the cloud of heads.   The Klucznik, passing,
Bowed, till he loosed him from the crush, and
　　said :

" Illustrious, Most Powerful Hetman of
The Crown, or General—the title is
A trifling matter—I Rembajlo am.
I stand at your command with this my Penknife,
That not from workmanship, nor from inscriptions,
Nor from the temper of its blade such glory,
Earned, that even you, Illustrious Powerful Sir,
Knew of it.   If it could but speak, maybe
It might say something tending to the praise
Ev'n of this ancient hand it served so long ;
Faithful, may Heaven be thanked, to Fatherland,
And to the lords of the Horeszko race,
Whose memory still is famous among men.
Mopanku ! seldom any district Writer
So deftly trims his pen, as this does heads.

'Twere long to reckon up. And ears and noses
Countless ! And on this Penknife is no notch,
And never any murderous deed has stained it.
Once only !—give him, Lord, eternal rest !—
An unarmed man, alas ! it once despatched.
But even that, God be my witness, was
Pro bono publico."

    " Well, show it here,"
Said General Dombrowski, laughing.   " But
It is a handsome Penknife, truly 'tis
A headsman's sword ! "   With great astonishment
He looked upon the rapier, and in turn
Showed it to all the other officers.
They proved it all, but scarcely one of them
Could lift this rapier.   It is said Dembinski,*
Renowned for strength of arm, might have upraised
This sabre, but he was not there.   Of those
Then present, only might Dwernicki, chief
Of squadron, and Rosycki, of platoon
Lieutenant, turn this iron pole around ;
And thus the rapier went from hand to hand,
In turn, on proof.
    But General Kniaziewicz,

---

* Leader first in the insurrection of 1831, later on in the
Hungarian war of 1848–49.

The most illustrious in stature, showed
That he was likewise strongest in the arm.
Holding the rapier lightly, as a sabre,
He raised it, and above all heads he made
Its lightnings gleam, remembering all the arts
Of Polish fencing, cross-stroke, mill, and curved
Stroke, stolen cut, and thrusts of contrapunt,
Of tercets, which he likewise understood,
For he was of the School of Cadets.

As
He fenced thus, laughing, did Rembajlo kneel,
Embrace him round the knees, and cry with
    tears,
At every turn the sword made : " Beautiful ;
Say, General, wert thou a Confederate ?
Most beautiful, most perfectly !   That is
Pulawski's thrust, thus Dzierzanowski stood.
That is the thrust of Sawa ![3] who thus formed
Your hand, except Matthias Dobrzynski?   But
That, General, is my invention.   Heaven
Forbid ! I do not praise myself !   That stroke
Is only in the *zascianek* known
Of the Rembajlos, from my name 'tis called
Mopanku's stroke.   Who taught it to you,
    sir ?

That is my own stroke, mine!" He rose, the
    General
Seizing in his embrace. "Now shall I die
In peace. There's yet upon the earth a man
Who will my dear child cherish! For indeed
Both day and night I long have sorely grieved,
Lest this my rapier rust when I am dead.
Behold, it shall not rust! My most Illustrious,
Most Powerful General, pardon me, throw off
Those *spits*, those German swords; to a noble child
'Twere shame to wear those sticks. Take here a
    sword
That suits a noble! This my Penknife I
Here lay before your feet, the dearest thing
That in the world I own. I never had
A wife, I have no child; it was to me
Both wife and child; it never left my arms.
From morn till twilight have I cherished it;
By night it slept beside me, and when I
Grew old, it on the wall hung o'er my couch,
As o'er a Jew the Lord's commandments. I
Have thought it should be buried in my grave,
Together with my hand. But I have found
An heir. Thee let it serve."
                     The General,

Half-laughing, with emotion half o'ercome,
"Comrade," he said, "if thou dost yield thy wife
And child to me, through thy remaining years
Thou wilt be very lonely, old and widower,
And childless.   Tell me, by what gift shall I
Repay thee, and by what thy childless state
And widowhood assuage?"—"Am I Cybulski?"[4]
The Klucznik said in grief, "who lost his wife,
At cards unto a Muscovite, the tale
The song relates?   It is enough for me,
That yet my Penknife shines before the world,
In such a hand.   But, General, remember
The sword-belt must be long, extended well,
For it is long, and aye from the left ear
Strike with both edges, so shalt thou cut through
From head to belly."
                     Then the General
The Penknife took, but since it was so long,
He could not wear it; so the servants laid it
Safe in the baggage waggon.   What of it
Became, concerning that were differing tales,
But none for certain knew, nor then, nor after.

Dombrowski said to Matthew, "How now, com-
    rade!

'Twould seem my coming does not much rejoice
    thee,
Silent and sour !   Why does thy heart not leap
To see the eagles, golden, silver, when
The trumpeters Kosciuszko's *réveille*
Sound in thine ears ?   Matthew, I thought thou wert
A bolder fellow !   If thou wilt not draw
Thy sabre, and on horseback mount, at least
Thou'lt drink with thy companions merrily
Unto Napoleon's and to Poland's health.

" Ha !" Matthew said, " I see what here is doing.
But, sir, two eagles may not nest together.
Lords' favour, Hetman, rides on piebald horse.*
The Emperor's a great warrior, much is there
To talk of.   I remember the Pulawskis,[5]
My friends, were used to say about Dumourier,[6]—
For Poland there must be a Polish hero,
No Frenchman, nor Italian, but a Piast ;[7]
Must be a John, a Joseph, or a Matthew.
E basta !   Army !   Polish 'tis, they say ;
But fusiliers, and sappers, grenadiers,
And cannoniers ; we hear more German titles

* " *Baska panska na pstrym koniu jedzie*"—a national
proverb.

Than native in this crowd.   Who understands this?
And there must also be among you Turks,
And Tartars, or schismatics, with no God
Or faith.   Myself I saw it! they assault
The women in the hamlets, rob the passers,
And   pillage   churches.   The   Emperor   goes   to
    Moscow.
A long way, if his Majesty the Emperor
Has made this undertaking without God.
I have heard he is already under curse
Of a bishop.   All this is "—here Matthew dipped
Bread in the soup, and eating, ended not
His sentence.

           Matthew's sayings did not please
The Chamberlain.   The younger folk besides
Began to murmur.   Then the Judge broke off
These quarrels, by proclaiming the arrival
Of the third pair betrothed.

              It was the Regent.
Himself proclaimed himself the Regent, else
None would have known him. Hitherto he had worn
The Polish costume, but now Telimena,
His future wife,[8] obliged him by a clause
Of marriage-contract to renounce the *kontusz.*
And so the Regent willy-nilly dressed

Himself in French costume.   Well might be seen
The *frac* had taken half his soul away.
He stept as he a stick had swallowed, straight,
Unmoving, like a crane ; he dared not look
To right or left ; he came with stately mien,
But from his mien one saw he suffered tortures.
He knew not how to bend, or where to place
His hands, who so loved gestures.   At his girdle
He would have placed his hands,—there was no
    girdle,
So he but stroked his waist.   He saw his error ;
And in confusion coloured fiery red,*
And in one pocket of the *frac* concealed
Both hands.   He stepped as though through rods,
    through whispers
And mockings, shame enduring for the *frac*,
As for an evil deed.   At last he met
The eyes of Matthew, and with fear he trembled.
Matthew till then had been the Regent's friend ;
Now on him such a sharp and savage glance
He turned, that pale the Regent grew, began
To fasten close his buttons, thinking Matthew
Would strip him of the *frac* by looks alone.

---

* The Polish original is striking, being literally, "roasted
a crab."

Dobrzynski only twice said loudly, "Fool!"
But such his anger at the Regent's dress,
That he at once from table rose, without
Leave-taking made his exit, and on horseback
Mounting, returned unto his farmstead home.

But in the meantime did the Regent's love,
Fair Telimena, all her beauty's splendours
And of her dress display, from head to foot
All in the newest fashion.   What her dress
Or head adornment seemed, 'twere vain to write;
The pen could not exhaust them, only might
The pencil trace those tulles, those blondes, cash-
        meres,
Those pearls and precious stones, and rosied
        cheeks,
And lively glances.
                        Instantly the Count
Had recognised her; with astonishment
All pale he rose from table, sought his sword.
"And is it thou?" he cried, "or do mine eyes
Deceive me?   Thou, who in my presence claspest
A stranger's hand?   O faithless being! thou
Most changeful soul!   Thou dost not hide with
        shame

Thy face beneath the earth? Thus art thou
    mindless
Of such late vows? How credulous I was!
Wherefore have I these ribbons worn? But woe
Unto the rival who affronts me thus!
He shall not to the altar pass, except
Upon my corpse."
              The guests arose, the Regent
Confounded greatly; to appease the rivals
The Chamberlain makes haste. But Telimena,
Leading the Count aside : " As yet," she whispered.
"The Regent has not taken me to wife.
If you will hinder it, pray tell me so.
But answer me at once, and in few words,
If you do love me ? have you hitherto
Not changed your heart? are you prepared to-day
To marry me? at once? to-day? and if
You will, I'll leave the Regent." Said the Count :
"O woman ! unto me not understood !
Once in thy sentiments thou wast a poet,
And now to me thou seemest nought but prose.
What are your marriages, if aught but chains,
That only fetter hands, and bind not souls?
Believe me, they are only declarations
Without confession; they are obligations,

Which bind not! Two hearts at the world's far
        ends
Burning, converse like stars with trembling beams.
Who knows? maybe for this cause towards the sun
The earth aye presses, and is therefore ever
So dear unto the moon; eternally
They gaze upon each other, and for aye
Haste by the shortest way each other toward,
But never can approach "—— " Enough of this,"
She interrupted; " I am not a planet!
For Heaven's sake enough, Count! I am a woman.
I know the rest already.   Cease to talk
To me of things not here nor there.   And now,
I warn you, if you whisper but one word
To break my wedding off, as true as God
In heaven is, I with these nails will spring
At you, and "—— " I will not," the Count replied,
" Madam, disturb your happiness."   He turned
Away his eyes all full of scorn and grief,
And as to punish his unfaithful love,
He took the daughter of the Chamberlain
For object of his steadfast fires.
                              The Wojski
Desired to make the angry youths agree
By wise examples; therefore he began

To adduce the wild-boar story in the woods
Of Naliboko, and of Rejtan's quarrel
With Prince Denassau.   But the guests meanwhile
Had left off eating ices, and they went
For coolness from the castle to the court.

There had the peasantry their feast concluded :
Pitchers of mead were circling round ; the music
Was tuning now, and calling to the dance.
They sought for Thaddeus, who stood apart,
And whispered something to his future wife :
" Sophia, I must now in a thing of weight
Take counsel with thee ; I have asked my uncle,
And he has no objection.   Thou dost know,
A large proportion of those villages
I shall possess, according to the law
Revert to thee ; these peasants are not mine,
They are thy subjects ; I should never dare
Dispose of them without their lady's will.
But when we have a Fatherland beloved,
Shall villagers enjoy this happy change
By so much only, that it gives to them
Another master ?   True it is, till now
They have been ruled with kindliness, but after
My death who knows how I shall leave them ?   I

A soldier am, and we are mortal both.
I am a man, I fear my own caprices.
More safely shall we do, if we renounce
Such rule, and give up the serfs' destiny
To the protection of the law.   Ourselves
Now free, let us the serfs make also free ;
Let us bestow on them in heritage
The holding of these lands where they were born,
That by a work of blood they have obtained.
But I must warn thee, that these lands bestowing
Our revenue will lessen, we must live
On moderate fortune.   I to frugal life
Am used from childhood ; but for thee, Sophia ?
Thou art of noble lineage, thou hast spent
Thy childhood in the capital ; canst thou
Agree to dwell here in the country, thus
Far from the world, and as a country woman ? "

To this Sophia answered modestly :
" I am a woman ; counsel unto me
Does not belong, and you will be my husband.
I am too young for counsel.   What you do,
To that I shall agree with all my heart.
If, Thaddeus, thou becomest poorer for
Delivering the serfs, thou wilt be all

The dearer to my heart.   I little know
About my lineage, and I little care
About it : I remember only this,
That I was a poor orphan, and adopted
By the Soplicas, as a daughter cherished
Within their house, and thence in marriage given.
I do not fear the country ; if I once
Lived in a great town, it is long ago,
I have forgotten it ;—I always loved
The country, and believe me, that my cocks
And hens amused me more than Petersburg ;
And if at times I longed for entertainments,
And company, it was from childishness ;
For now I know the city wearies me.
Last winter a short stay in Wilna taught me
That I was born for country life.   Amid
Amusements still I longed for Soplicowo.
Nor fear I work, for I am young and strong ;
I know how to go round the house, and how
To carry keys, and thou shalt see how I
Will learn housekeeping."
                              When Sophia had spoken
These last words, came towards her the astonished
And sour Gervasy.   "I know all," he said.
" The Judge has spoken of this liberty.

But yet I do not understand what this
Can have to do with serfs.   I fear me lest
'Tis something German.   Liberty indeed
Is not a thing for peasants, but for nobles.
'Tis true that we from Adam all descend;
But I have heard that peasants come from Ham,[9]
The Jews from Japhet, we nobility
From Shem, and thus as elders rule o'er both;
Yet otherwise the parish priest now teaches.
He says that it has been so formerly,
And in the ancient dispensation; but
When Christ our Lord, though He from kings
        descended,
Was born among the Jews in peasants' stable,
He levelled all ranks, and made them agree.
And so thus let it be, if it may not
Be otherwise!   Above all, as I hear,
My lady, most Illustrious and Powerful,
Sophia, does agree to all.   'Tis hers
To give command, mine to obey.   But only
I warn you, let us give not merely empty
And verbal freedom,[10] as among the Russians,
When Pan Karp late deceased did free his serfs,
And with a triple tax the Muscovites
Brought them to famine.   Therefore I advise

That by an ancient custom we ennoble
The peasants, and proclaim we give to them
Our crest.   My lady on some villages
Confer her Half-goat, Pan Soplica share
The Leliwa with others.   That once done,
Rembajlo owns the peasant as his equal,
When he beholds him nobleman, Most Powerful,
With coat-of-arms.   The Diet will confirm it.

" But let my lady's husband have no fear
That giving of the lands will make you poor.
Forbid it, heaven ! that I should ever see
The hands of daughter of a dignitary
Cumbered with household labours.   There are
    means
To hinder this.   I know a treasure-chest
Within the castle, which contains the plate
Of the Horeszkos, likewise signet-rings,
Medals and jewels, and rich plumes and trappings
Of horses, wondrous sabres, treasure of
The Pantler, in the ground preserved from plunder.
Lady Sophia as inheritrix
Possesses it.   I watched it in the castle,
As 'twere the apple of my eye I kept it
From Russians, and from you, Soplicas too.

I have a great bag full of mine own ducats
Besides, collected from my salaries,
Also from gifts of lords.   I thought whene'er
The castle was restored to us, to use
The money for repairing of the walls :
To-day for the new housekeeping it seems
Useful at last.   Then, Pan Soplica, I
Transfer myself to your house, in my lady's
I'll live upon the bread of favour, cradling
From the Horeszkos the third generation,
And to the Penknife mould my lady's child,
If 'tis a son ;—but it a son will be ;
For wars are coming, and in time of war
Those born are always sons."

                                  Gervasy scarce
These last words spake, when with slow, solemn steps
Approached Protasy.   Bowing low, from forth
The bosom of his *kontusz* he produced
A monstrous panegyric,[11] written on
Two folios and a half.   It was composed
In rhyme by a young under-officer,
Who in the capital had formerly
Written some famous odes, and then put on
The uniform ; but being in the army
Still a belle-lettrist, he made verses still.

The Wozny now had read three hundred through ;
Till coming to this place, "O thou whose charms
Wake painful bliss and rapturous alarms,
When on Bellona's ranks thy countenance
Thou turnest, straight are shivered sword and
     lance ;
Let Hymen vanquish Mars, and haste to tear
From Discord's front the hissing vipers there "—
Sophia and Thaddeus clapped unceasingly,
As though they praised it, in reality
Not wishing to hear more.   Already by
Commandment of the Judge the parish priest
Upon the table mounted, and proclaimed
The will of Thaddeus to the peasantry.

Scarcely the serfs had heard this news, they sprang
To their young lord, fell at their lady's feet.
" Health to our lord and lady !" they exclaimed,
With tears.   " Health to our fellow-citizens,"
Cried Thaddeus; "free and equal! Poles !" "I give
The People's health !" Dombrowski said.   The
     people
Cried out, " Long live the generals ! long live
The army ! live the people ! all the states !"
With thousand voices rang alternate healths.

Alone deigned Buchman not to share this joy;
He praised the project, but would gladly see it
Quite otherwise, and first appoint a legal
Commission which should——

> Shortness of the time

Prevented justice doing to Buchman's counsel;
For in the castle courtyard stood already
Couples for dancing; officers with ladies,
The common soldiers with the peasant women.
"A Polonaise!" all cried out with one voice.
The officers had brought the army music,
But the Judge whispered to the General:
"Give orders, sir, the band shall yet stay back.
This day is the betrothal of my nephew,
And 'tis an ancient custom of our house
To be betrothed and wed to village music.
Look, here the cymbalist, the fiddler stand,
And piper;—honest folks! the fiddler now
Stands eager, and the piper bows, entreating
With glance of eyes.   Should I them send away,
They'd weep, poor fellows.   And the people cannot
Spring to another music.   Let them now
Begin, and let the people all rejoice,
And later on we'll hear your chosen band."
He gave the sign.

The fiddler of his coat
Tucked up the sleeves, he tightly grasped the neck,
Upon the fiddle-head he leaned his chin,
And like a horse in full career set off
Upon the fiddle; at this sign the pipers,
Who stood beside, as though they flapped with
    wings,
With frequent motion of their shoulders blow
Into the bags, and fill their cheeks with breath.
Thou might'st have thought the pair would fly away
Upon the air, like Boreas' wingèd children.
Cymbals were wanting.

               Cymbalists were many;
But none dared play while Jankiel was near.
Where Jankiel tarried all the winter through
None knew; now all at once he had appeared
With the chief army staff.   All knew that none
Were equal to him on this instrument
In taste and talent.   They entreated he
Would play, presented cymbals, but the Jew
Refused, and said his hands were coarsened, he
Was out of practice, dared not, was ashamed
To play before the gentlemen; he bowed,
And went away.   When this Sophia saw,
She ran up to him, and in her white hand

The bars wherewith the master sounds the strings
She offered ; with the other hand she stroked
The old man's hoary beard, and curtsying,
" Do, Jankiel," says she, " if you please, to-day
Is my betrothal, Jankiel, do play ;
You have promised oft to play upon my wedding."

As Jankiel loved Sophia exceedingly,
He nodded with his chin, in sign he did not
Refuse, and so they led him to their midst.
They gave to him a chair, they bring the cymbals,
And place them on his knees.   He looks with joy
And pride on them, like veteran called to arms,
Whose grandsons from the wall his heavy sword
Drag down ; the old man laughs, although so long
No sword was in his hand, yet has he felt
The hand is yet no stranger to the sword.

Meanwhile two scholars by the cymbals kneel,
Attune the strings once more, and tuning strike.
Jankiel is silent yet, with half-shut eyes,
And still his fingers grasp the unmoving bars.[12]

He let them go.   At first they beat the time
Of a triumphal march ; more frequent, then

They smote along the strings like stormy rain.
All marvelled.   But this only was as proof ;
For soon he broke off, and aloft he raised
Both bars.

     He played again.   The bars vibrate
With such light motion, as a fly's wing might
Upon the chords, emitting a low hum,
Scarce heard.   The master ever looked towards
  heaven,
Awaiting inspiration.   From above
He looked, the instrument with proud glance
  scanned.
He raised his hands together, dropped, and smote
With those two bars.   The hearers marvelled much.

From many strings together burst a sound,
As a whole band of Janissary music
Awoke with bells, with *zel*,* and beating drums ;
The Polonaise of May the third.   The lively
Maidens breathe hard with joy, the lads may scarce
Stay in their places.   But the old men's thoughts
Were with the sound transported to the past,
Into those happy years when deputies

---

  * An eastern instrument : *vide* " Lallah Rookh."

And senators upon the third of May,
In the town-hall did feast the king, made one
Now with the nation, when in dance they sung :
" Long live the King, the Diet live, the Estates, the
    Nation long ! "
The master hurries evermore the time,
Intensifies the tones ; but at that instant
Threw in a false chord like a serpent's hiss,
Or scratch of iron on glass ; all horror seized,
And all their joy an evil-boding fear
Confounded, saddened, frightened all the hearers.
They doubted : was the instrument mistuned ?
In error the musician ?   Such a master
Could not mistake.   He purposely has stirred
Again that traitorous string, the melody
Is troubled ; ever louder, breaketh in
That chord unbridled, all confederate
Against the concord of the other tones.
At last the Klucznik understood the master ;
He covered with his face his hands, and cried :
" I know, I know that sound, 'tis Targowica ! "
And presently that string ill-boding burst
With hissing.

        The musician to the treble
Rushes, he breaks the time, confuses it.

He leaves the treble, rushes to the bass ;
And evermore and louder still are heard
A thousand uproars ; beating of a march,
Of war, assault, and storm ; then shots were heard,
The groans of children, and their mothers weeping.
The perfect master so the horrors gave
Of storming, that the village women trembled ;
Recalling to themselves, with tears of pain,
The Praga carnage, which they knew from songs
And stories.   Glad they were that suddenly
The master thundered loud with all the strings,
And strangled all the voices, as though he
Had beat them to the ground.

      The hearers scarce
Had time to issue from astonishment ;
Again another music ; once again
At first a humming light and low, there sigh
Some slender strings, like flies, who strive to loose
Themselves from nets of spiders.   But the chords
Increase aye more and more.   The scattered tones
Unite, and legions gather of accords ;
And now, with sounds accordant, move in time,
The tune creating of that famous song,
Of how the soldier over hills and forests
Goeth, at times well-nigh with hunger dying,

Falling at last before his charger's feet,
Who with his foot shall dig for him a grave,
The ancient song to Poland's army dear.[13]
The soldiers knew it ; all the faithful ranks
Gathered around the master, listening.
They to themselves recall that fearful time,
When o'er their country's grave they sang that song,
And went into the country of the world.*
In thought they track their years of wandering,
O'er lands, o'er seas, through burning sands and frost,
Amid strange peoples, where so oft in camp
This native song rejoiced and heartened them.
Thus thinking, sadly they bowed down their heads.

But soon they raised them.   For the master raised
The tones, intensified and changed the time,
Proclaiming somewhat else ; he scanned the strings,
He joined his hands, and smote with both the bars.
So artful was the stroke, and of such power,
That the strings sounded forth like brazen trumpets,
And from the trumpets the triumphal march
Rolled toward the sky, "Yet Poland is not dead !
Dombrowski ! march to Poland !" and all clapped,

---

* A common equivalent for into the wide world.

And all in chorus, " March ! Dombrowski !" cried.
The master, as though marvelling at his song,
Dropped from his hands the bars, and raised his
     hands
On high ; his cap of fox-skin from his head
Fell on his shoulders, and his reverend beard
Waved, lifted high ; upon his cheek there stood
Circles of wondrous red, and in his glance
All full of spirit, shone the glow of youth.
Till when the old man turned his eyes upon
Dombrowski, with his hands he covered them ;
Beneath his hands a flood of tears poured forth.
" General !" he cried, " long has our Litva waited
For thee, as we Jews our Messiah await !
Long singers 'mid the people have foretold thee,
And heaven proclaimed thee by a miracle !
Live thou, and fight !—Oh! thou, our"—speaking he
Kept sobbing, for the honest Jew our country
Loved like a Pole.   Dombrowski gave his hand
To him, and thanked him.   He, his cap removed,
Did kiss the leader's hand.
      The Polonaise
Shall now begin.   The Chamberlain does rise,
And lightly throwing back his *kontusz* cuffs,
And twirling his moustache, presents his hand

Unto Sophia, and bowing courteously
Invites her into the first couple.   Following
The Chamberlain, there forms a rank in pairs.
The signal given, the dance begins; he leads.

Upon the turf the red boots shine, there gleams
A lustre from the sabre, the rich girdle
Shines brightly ; but he slowly steps as though
Unwilling : but from every step, each motion,
The dancer's thoughts and feelings may be read.
See, now he stands, as he would ask his lady ;
He bends towards her, whispers in her ear ;
The lady turns her head away, seems bashful,
She listens not ; he takes his cap off, bends
Humbly ; the lady deigns to cast a glance,
But keeps a silence obstinate ; he tracks
Her glances with his eyes, and laughs at length,
Glad of her answer ; quicker steps he forth,
Looks down upon his rivals ; and his cap,
With heron's plumes, now on his brow suspends,
Now shakes it o'er his forehead, till he lays it
Upon one side, and twirls round his moustache.
He goes, all envy him, rush on his traces ;
He gladly with his lady would escape
Out of the crowd, at times stands in his place,

And courteously he lifts his hand, and that
They would approach him humbly doth entreat.
At times he thinks with skill to turn aside,
Changeth the path, glad to mislead the rest ;
But with swift step importunate they follow.
So he grows angry, and his right hand lays
Upon his sword-hilt, while he seems to say,
" I care not for you ! to the envious woe ! "
He turns, with pride upon his brow, and with
Defiance in his eye, straight through the crowd ;
The crowd of dancers dare not him approach,
They yield to him the way, and change their ranks ;
Once more pursuing him.

               And loud applause
Resounds on all sides : " Ah ! that is the last,
Maybe ! look, look, young people, 'tis perhaps
The last who thus can lead a Polonaise ! "
And pairs still followed pairs with noise and joy.
The circle now unwound, now wound again,
Like to a giant snake in thousand folds,
And change the varied, many hues of dresses
Of ladies, lords, and soldiers, like its scales
Gleaming, and gilded by the western sun,
On the dark cushion of the turf.   The dance
Is seething, music sounding, healths and plaudits.

Alone the Corporal Dobrzynski Bustard
Hears not the band, nor dances, nor rejoices.
With hands behind his back he standeth, cross
And gloomy, thinking of his former suit
Unto Sophia, how he loved to bring her
Flowers, weave her baskets, capture birds' nests,
    carve
Earrings! Ungrateful girl! Although he lavished
So many gifts upon her, though she fled
Before him, though his father did forbid him,
He yet—how often on the garden wall
He sat, to gaze while she her garden weeded,
Or gathered cucumbers, or cockerels fed!
Ungrateful girl! He drooped his head at last;
He whistled a mazurka, then he pressed
The hat upon his ears, and to the camp
He went, where stood the watch beside the guns.
There to distract his mind he played at draughts
With soldiers, with the bowl his grief assuaged.
Such, for Sophia, Dobrzynski's constancy.

Sophia dances joyously, but though
In the first couple, scarcely seen from far.
On the green surface of the courtyard wide,
In dress of green adorned with field-flowers, and

In flowery garland, 'mid the flowers and grasses
She circles round, in flight invisible,
The dance directing as an angel guides
The course of nightly stars.   Thou guessest where
She is, for all the eyes are turned towards her,
All arms are stretched forth, towards her all the
    crowd
Do press.   The Chamberlain in vain does strive
To stay beside her; envious men have now
Repulsed him from the first place, and the happy
Dombrowski might not long rejoice himself,
But yield her to another; and a third
Already hastened, and this one repulsed,
At once departed hopeless.   Then Sophia,
Already wearied out, met Thaddeus
In turn, and fearful of a further change,
And wishing to remain with him, she ended
The dances, and towards the table went
To fill up goblets for the guests.
                         The sun
Had set already; warm the evening was,
And stilly; heaven's circle here and there
Was paved with clouds, above of bluish hue,
Rosy towards the west; these clouds forebode
Fine weather, light and shining; there like flock

Of sheep that slumber on the grass, and there
Are lesser clouds like flocks of water-fowl;
And in the west a cloud like veily curtains,
Transparent, in deep folds; above like pearl,
Upon the borders gilded; in its depths
Of purple hue; yet with the western blaze
It sparkled, and it glowed, till gradually
It grew more yellow, paler, and then grey.
The sun has drooped his head, the cloud removed,
And giving one sigh with the warm air, slept.
But evermore the nobles drink, with healths
Unto Napoleon, to the generals,
To Thaddeus and Sophia, and at last
In turn of all three couples then betrothed,
Of all the guests there present, all invited,
All friends whom living any one recalled,
And those now dead whose memory was holy.

And I myself was there among the guests: [14]
I drank the wine and mead, and what I saw
And heard there I have written in a book.

NOTES TO BOOK XII.

1. "*But in the meantime the great service changed.*"

* In the sixteenth and at the beginning of the seventeenth century, at the time when art was most flourishing, even banquets were arranged by artists, and full of symbols and theatrical devices. At the renowned festival given in Rome to Leo X. was a service representing in turn the four seasons of the year, which probably served as the model for that of Radziwill. These table customs were changed in Europe about the middle of the eighteenth century : they lasted longest in Poland.

2.   " *Has Pineti*
Given you his devils for your service? "

* Pineti, a magician renowned through all Poland ; when he was among us we do not know.

3. " *Dzierzanowski . . . Sawa.*"

Dzierzanowski and the Cossack Sawa were both famous as heroes of the Confederacy.

4.   " ' *Am I Cybulski?* '
The Klucznik said in grief."

* The lamentation of the wife of Cybulski, whose husband lost her at cards to a Muscovite, is well known in Lithuania.

5. " *The Pulawskis.*"

The five Pulawskis, father, three brothers, and nephew, were all distinguished in the Confederacy of Bar, formed to resist Russian interference ; being its first originators and afterwards its life and soul. After the death of his father Casimir Pulawski became chief of the whole Confederacy, maintained it for a long time, and was at length persuaded to accede to the seizure of King Stanislas in Warsaw. This act has been undeservedly reprobated by a once famous English novelist, but it was certainly ill-judged, for it contributed to the loss of *prestige* in the Confederates, and the downfall of their cause. After the ruin of the Confederacy Pulawski fought for some time in Turkey against the Russians, and subsequently taking part in the American War of Independence, fell in an assault on Fort Wayne (1779).

6. " *To say about Dumourier.*"

Several French officers, chiefly Dumourier, also Choiseul Vismenil, and others, took part with the Confederates.

7. " *A Piast.*"

A Piast originally signified a sovereign of the first historic dynasty that reigned over Poland, from Piast, the reputed founder of the race, to Casimir the Great, who died in 1370. In later times, during the period of elected sovereigns, a Piast came to mean a king, or candidate for the throne, of Polish birth. Hence it is here used for a national hero.

8. " *His future wife,*" &c.

* The fashion of dressing in the French style increased greatly in the provinces between the years 1800 to 1812.

Young men often changed their style of dress before marriage, at the request of their betrothed.

9. "*But I have heard the peasants come from Ham.*"

We may notice this curious coincidence (a very unscriptural genealogy, by the way) between these ideas and the reasons alleged by the Southerners for keeping the negroes in slavery. The reader will remember that the word "Cham" is actually used earlier in the poem in addressing a peasant.

10. "*Not merely empty and verbal freedom.*"

* The Russian Government acknowledged no freemen except nobles. Serfs, freed by their proprietors, were at once inscribed among the peasants of the Imperial estates, and instead of compulsory labour were forced to pay increased taxes. It is well known that in the year 1818 the inhabitants of the governorship of Wilna decreed in the Senate a project of freeing all the serfs, and appointed for this purpose a delegation to the Emperor ; but the government ordered the project to be hushed up, and nevermore to be fmentioned. There was no way of freeing a man at that time, under Russian rule, except by adopting him into the family. Therefore many were freed in this way, either by avour or for money.

11. "*A monstrous panegyric.*"

Before the inauguration of a better taste by Mickiewicz and other great writers, the so-called French or Classical school of literature in Poland produced a quantity of *panegyrics* or complimentary verses in honour of great personages, with stale classical images, and strained, far-fetched metaphors, destitute of real poetry. Our author has seized this happy opportunity of satirising the faults of classicism.

12. " *He grasped the unmoving bars.* "

" The cymbals are a species of lyre laid flat on a table, and played with padded sticks. They have great tone and capability of expression, and emit as much sound as a grand piano ; the lower strings have immense depth and power."— " *Unknown Hungary,*" *by a Member of the Carpathian Club.*

13. " *The ancient song,* " &c.

The opening words of this song are nearly as quoted in the text. The melody is of a plaintive and melancholy character. It is included in Sowinski's collection of national music, published at Paris.

14. " *And I myself,*" &c.

With these few concluding words the poet indicates his own presence at the concluding festivities, and personal cognisance of all the circumstances related. We are reminded of Chaucer's parenthetical phrase in the Prologue to the Canterbury Tales, " and then there was myself, there was no mo." The conclusion is, however, probably meant to imitate the general ending of Polish fairy tales, which commonly finish as this poem does, by a sort of rhyming couplet, assuring us that the narrator was himself present at the wedding-feast, and shared in the festivities.

THE END.

PRINTED BY BALLANTYNE, HANSON AND CO.
EDINBURGH AND LONDON.

www.ingramcontent.com/pod-product-compliance
Lightning Source LLC
Chambersburg PA
CBHW060615030726
47498CB00005B/1680